BFF'S 2:

Best Frenemies Forever Series

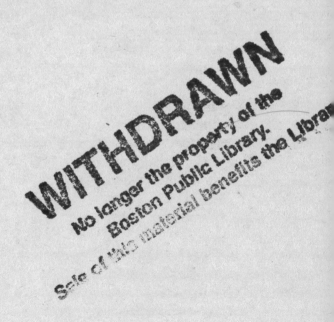

BFF'S 2:

Best Frenemies Forever Series

Brenda Hampton

URBAN BOOKS

www.urbanbooks.net

Urban Books, LLC
97 N18th Street
Wyandanch, NY 11798

BFF'S 2: Best Frenemies Forever Series
Copyright © 2015 Brenda Hampton

ISBN 13: 978-1-62286-791-2
ISBN 10: 1-62286-791-2

First Mass Market Printing February 2017
First Trade Paperback Printing February 2015
Printed in the United States of America

10 9 8 7 6 5 4 3 2 1

This is a work of fiction. Any references or similarities to actual events, real people, living or dead, or to real locales are intended to give the novel a sense of reality. Any similarity in other names, characters, places, and incidents is entirely coincidental.

Distributed by Kensington Publishing Corp.
Submit Orders to:
Customer Service
400 Hahn Road
Westminster, MD 21157-4627
Phone: 1-800-733-3000
Fax: 1-800-659-2436

Chapter 1

Kayla

I was a nervous wreck. Jacoby's phone call about Cedric being shot had me driving like a bat out of the devil's lonely hell. I swerved in and out of traffic, trying to get to the place I once called home. Tears streamed down my face. I could barely see the road through my blurred vision. My heart raced like I was on the verge of a heart attack, and so many thoughts swarmed in my head.

No matter what Cedric had done to destroy our marriage, I didn't want him to die. He had been the worst husband ever, but in no way did I want to be a widow. I still had much love for him. Someway or somehow, I thought we could piece our marriage back together. But after today, that would be difficult. If he survived his injuries, I didn't know how I would be able to forgive him for having a relationship with my best friend,

Evelyn. How could I forgive the lies and betrayal of what they'd done? It wouldn't be easy, but for now, I had to focus on Cedric.

When I spoke to Jacoby earlier, he said that someone called 911 and the police and ambulance were on their way. I couldn't stop thinking about who could've wanted to kill Cedric. Why would they want him dead? I had my issues with him, no doubt, but I'd never thought about killing him. I should have, though, especially after the way he treated me; kicking me out of the house, removing money from my bank account, and fucking my friend—that was a sure way to get me stirred up.

I couldn't say that I was totally surprised by Evelyn's announcement today, but I couldn't get that smirk she'd had on her face, while making her confession, off my mind. We were at Trina's apartment, and Evelyn claimed to have something on her mind that she needed to say.

"I don't know where to start," Evelyn said. I wanted to slap her. "But I owe you an apology too. This is so hard for me to say, but as your best friend, I have betrayed you."

I was so out of it because of an earlier conversation I'd had with Cedric. He admitted to not loving me anymore, and for the first time, I was convinced that he wanted our marriage to end.

The affairs hadn't convinced me, but hearing him say he'd fallen out of love did. While in a daze, listening to my so-called BFF, I bit my nails and stared straight ahead. I mumbled a bunch of hateful words underneath my breath then spoke clearly so that Trina and Evelyn could hear me.

"I . . . I saw you at my house today," I stuttered, referring to seeing Evelyn. "I went there to get Cedric to change his mind about our divorce, but he didn't want to do it. He said that he didn't love me anymore. I can't believe that he . . . just . . . does not love . . . me . . . anymore."

There was no question that I was out of it. Knowing that my marriage had failed really hurt, but my hurt was about to sting even more. I could feel it, especially since Evelyn appeared ready to spill her guts. Her news would surely send me over the edge, and I wouldn't have wished this feeling on my worst enemy.

"What have you seen going on between him and Evelyn?" Trina was trying hard to get me to come to the light. "When you stopped by his house, did you see anything? You had to see something."

I rubbed my hands together and stood. As I paced the floor, I squeezed my aching forehead then wrapped my arms around my waist to comfort myself. "I didn't see anything today, but something is going on. I can feel it. You know how you have this eerie feeling inside that something is wrong? He said Evelyn was there for money, but I think there's more to it. I really do, but I can't put my finger on it."

"Well, put your finger on it and touch it," Trina shouted.

I was rattled by her loud mouth, but why didn't she just tell me? She knew. All along, she knew what the hell had been going on behind my back.

She continued, "Open your eyes and see it. What are you feeling? Say it, Kayla. Don't be afraid to say it and don't lie to yourself anymore. Don't ignore what you know. Your gut has been telling you things, but you've been ignoring it. Rewind the tape and play those images in your head. Ask yourself: what do you see?"

I removed my arms from my waist and slowly shut my eyes. A flood of tears cascaded down my face. It was time for me to release all that I'd felt inside, and when I opened my eyes, I did. They locked right on Evelyn who sat with glee in her eyes, waiting for my response.

"I see Cedric and I see you, Evelyn. I've seen the way he looks at you, and I've seen the way you smile at him. I saw him at your place one day." I paused to suck in a deep breath, and then I released it. *"And . . . and I saw your earrings and nasty panties in his car. I saw his account where he transferred thousands and thousands of dollars into your account, and I . . . I smell the scent of my husband when I walk into your home. So the questions are: Are you fucking my husband? If so, why didn't either of my best friends tell me what in the hell has been going on behind my back?"*

I could sense Evelyn's fakeness. She swallowed hard and sat with teary eyes. After blinking to wash away her tears, she scooted to the edge of the couch. "I'll answer your question, but for the record, you have never seen my nasty panties in Cedric's car. Those panties must have belonged to someone else. As I said before, I do owe you an apology—not for fucking your husband, but for allowing him to fuck me and use me to hurt you. For that, I am deeply sorry. I truly hope that you will one day forgive me for interfering in your marriage when I shouldn't have."

The room fell silent. I gazed at her without a blink and was ready to beat that bitch's ass! But for whatever reason, I couldn't move. I couldn't open my mouth. All I could do was stare in disbelief. I wanted to be wrong about the two of them, but her acknowledging the affair proved me right. Seconds later, my cell phone rang. It was Jacoby, crying hysterically and telling me that Cedric had been shot.

After Jacoby's call, I left in a hurry. I was on my way to see what was up. My car was moving at high speeds, but I needed to call Jacoby, again, to see what was going on. Unfortunately, he didn't answer. I called back several times, but got no response. I was only fifteen minutes away from Cedric's place, but I needed to know his condition. I needed to know if Jacoby was okay. Maybe he had done something to Cedric. They didn't get along that well, and these last few months had been hell for all of us. I hoped that he hadn't done anything this horrific, and the thought of it made my stomach turn. I was in deep thought, until I heard loud sirens. When I looked on the other side of the highway, a speeding ambulance had zoomed through traffic. That wasn't good. Was Cedric's dead body in there? Were the paramedics working hard to keep him alive? More tears fell, and I prayed all the way to my destination.

Upon arrival, I could see several police cars and plenty of my neighbors standing outside being nosy. Yellow crime scene tape squared the well-kept property and no one was allowed to cross the line. The front door was wide open. And when I looked around for Jacoby, he was nowhere in sight. I jerked the car in park and rushed to the first officer I saw. My legs wobbled and my heart raced faster, as I pulled on the officer's arm to get his attention.

"Where is my husband . . . my son? Please tell me what happened."

The officer could see how unstable I was. He pulled me closer to the house, as my neighbor, Betty, shouted to ask if I was okay.

"I hope so, and let us know how Cedric is. Meanwhile, please get Rich out of this. He didn't do anything but try to help, but the police keep questioning him."

I frowned because I was clueless to what she was talking about. That was until I looked into the back of a police car and saw her husband, Rich, sitting on the back seat while talking to an officer who sat in the front. Jacoby was inside of another car, and in another car was a white woman with dingy, blond hair. Her head hung low, and I couldn't see her face.

The officer held my arm and shook it. "Do you need an ambulance?" he said.

I shook my head, trying to come out of the daze I was in. "No, no, I don't. I need to find out what has happened to my husband, and why is my son in the back of the police car? I need to go see him."

I turned to walk away, but the officer grabbed my arm. "Come inside for a few minutes. If you're Mrs. Thompson, I need to speak to you."

"But I . . . I need to go see about my son. Why is he in the police car?"

"He's just speaking to one of the officers about what he saw. He'll be fine."

I moved my head from side to side and snatched away from the officer. I wasn't sure why he was trying to keep me away from Jacoby, and with him being seventeen the police had no right to question him without my consent. I stormed away from the aggressive officer who followed after me.

"Ma'am, I need to speak to you about your husband."

That got my attention, so I swung around to address him. "My husband? Where is he? Would someone please tell me where he's at?" I pounded my leg and started to cry even more.

"He's on his way to the hospital. We don't know his condition yet, but he was pretty bad when he left here in the ambulance."

I held my chest, squeezing it. That was when Jacoby got out of the police car and came up to me. He appeared frightened. The confusing look washed across his face upset me.

"Mama, this . . ." He paused to embrace me. And as my son who stood six two held me, he started to break down on me. "What has happened to our family?" he cried. "I thought you were the one who shot my dad, but I was wrong. I pray to God that he lives. God, please don't let him die. This is all my fault because I wished him dead, Mama. I prayed for his demise."

I looked around at the officers who were tuned in to Jacoby's every word. I didn't want him to incriminate himself, so I told him to be quiet. I rubbed his back and did my best to comfort him, considering how messed up I was.

"This is not your fault. I had my issues with Cedric too, but neither of us wanted him dead. As for our family, we'll be fine. Trust me, we will be fine, so don't you worry, okay?"

Jacoby nodded and backed away from me. He smacked tears away from his face then wiped down it with his hand to clear it.

"Rich saw her do it," he said. "He told me she did it, and I could've stopped her, Mama. I figured she would do something like this, especially after I talked to her that day."

My mind was going a mile a minute, trying to figure out what Jacoby was saying. But I couldn't comprehend anything because the officer behind me kept taking notes, and grabbing at my arm, asking me to come into the house. More sirens kept blaring, as more cars showed up. My nosy neighbors looking on didn't help either, and why were everybody's dogs barking? Maybe it was a good thing for us to go into the house, after Jacoby cleared himself of any wrongdoing.

I turned to the officer. "Officer, I will answer any question that you want me to, after I'm done speaking to my son. You say my husband is at the hospital, so we need to get there soon. Please allow me to get out of here to go see about him."

"Yes, we do need to get out of here," Jacoby said. "I'll fill you in, in the car and tell about what happened. But for now, let's go to the hospital to see what's up with my dad."

For whatever reason, the officer didn't want us to leave. "I'll arrive at the hospital in about thirty minutes," he said. "Hopefully, we'll be able to talk in private then."

"Sure," was all I said then rushed to my car with Jacoby.

On our way to the car, I took another glance at the white woman sitting in the police car with her head hung low. This time, two officers stood outside of the car, talking. I could barely see her, but when she swooped her frizzy hair behind her ears, my eyes grew wide. My mouth dropped open, and then I squinted to be sure that the woman was Cedric's receptionist, Paula Daniels. As I started to move in her direction, Jacoby called out to me.

"Let's go, Mama. Cedric needs us. I will tell you all about her in a minute."

I kept my eyes on her then slowly got into the car. As I drove off, she turned her head to look at me. Our eyes stayed connected, until she rolled hers and lowered her head again.

"Keep your eyes on the road, please," Jacoby said. "We will discuss her, but before we do, I want to ask if you're okay. You seem a little off."

"That's because I am. It's been a crazy day. The truth is, I don't know if I'm coming or going."

"I understand exactly how you feel. But before we get to the hospital, I need to tell you that Paula was the one who attempted to kill Cedric. She's been seeing him for quite some time, and he pushed her to the edge. He kicked her out of the house he purchased for her, and he also made promises to her that he failed to keep. I saw them together, numerous times—more recently in a parking garage getting it on. After that, I reached out to her. She told me what Cedric had done to her, and she threatened to kill him. I didn't take her seriously, but I should have.

"When I got home today, all I saw was Cedric's bloody body on a gurney. I thought he was dead, and at first, I assumed you had killed him. Forgive me for thinking that, but I knew how upset you were with him too. The truth is, Rich witnessed Paula walking toward our house with a shotgun in her hand. He followed her and called the police. By then, it was too late. Cedric had already been shot."

I was speechless. So much anger was inside of me. I couldn't believe that Cedric had been also having an affair with the receptionist, and then to buy her a house was crazy. I guess that explained why she always looked at me with envy in her eyes whenever I visited his office. It explained why she always had an attitude when I called to speak to him, and it explained why he always worked late hours. Then there were the Christmas parties, the company picnics, and the company milestones and celebration parties I attended with Cedric. I could always sense how fake Paula was. Deep inside, I always felt as if she was watching me, and for some reason, she seemed to hate me. I questioned Cedric about her attitude toward me, but he claimed that she treated everyone that way. He made it seem as if Paula had been dating one of his partners, not him. I believed him because she didn't seem like his type. But then again, what was Cedric's type? I really didn't know because me, Paula, and Evelyn were like night and day.

Thinking about all of this, yet again, I felt like a fool. First Evelyn, now Paula. I was starting to feel as if Cedric dying wouldn't be such a bad thing after all.

"Mama, I know what you're over there thinking, but you may want to speed it up so that we can get to the hospital. Going twenty miles an hour, we'll never get there."

"All of a sudden, I feel as if there is no rush. I hate to say this, but Cedric had this coming. I don't wish him bad, but you must understand how betrayed I feel. And his receptionist hasn't been the only woman. I just found out that he's been screwing Evelyn too."

Jacoby sat quiet. He looked straight ahead then lowered his head to look at his lap.

I slammed my hand on the steering wheel. "Please tell me that you didn't know about that too. Did you know that he'd been seeing Evelyn?"

There was a crisp silence for a few seconds then Jacoby spoke up. "Yes, I knew. Found out awhile back. I confronted her about her actions too, but she didn't see things my way. I wanted to tell you but, as your son, I didn't want to see you hurt. I felt relieved about the divorce, but you kept pushing to make things work. Then there was a part of me that wanted things to work out, too, because our family means everything to me."

I felt horrible inside. I understood how Jacoby felt, but no words could express how disgusted I was about the whole thing. Everybody had been keeping secrets from me, including my other friend, Trina, and now my own son. Something inside of me wanted to turn this car around, park it somewhere, and get the hell out of dodge.

"If you knew about Cedric's affair with Evelyn, I wish you would have said something. I always had my suspicions too, but it seems as if everyone wanted me to make a complete fool of myself. When I kept defending Cedric, all you had to do was tell me what he'd been up to."

"I did tell you." Jacoby raised his voice. "But you wouldn't listen, remember? I may not have been specific about Evelyn, but I told you Cedric was no good. I told you he'd been with other women, but all you did was yell at me. You told me that I was the one who needed to get my act together."

Jacoby shut me up with the quickness. He had mentioned Cedric's cheating ways to me before, but I chose to believe him and take his word that he wasn't cheating. I apologized to Jacoby. After that, I kept my mouth shut until we got to the hospital. Meanwhile, my thoughts about Cedric weren't good.

The hospital's emergency room was jam-packed. Two young men had been shot, and their families were all over the place, having a fit and praying to God for Him to save them. A child with a broken arm stood next to his mother in tears, and as she did her best to comfort him, a man in a wheelchair rolled in complaining about chest pains. I had already asked the nurse behind the counter where Cedric was, but all she said was for me to have a seat. When I pushed, she got antsy.

"Ma'am, all I can say right now is they're working on him. Please have a seat. The doctor will be with you shortly."

"Shortly as in a few minutes or a few hours? That's my husband back there. I would really like to know how he's doing."

I could see the young woman's eye twitch. "I repeat, the doctor will be with you shortly. There is nothing else that I can say right now."

I rolled my eyes and walked away. Jacoby walked next to me, and we both took seats in the waiting area. Even with a leather jacket on, I was cold. I had gotten all of my hair cut off earlier, and the short cut that I sported surely didn't keep my head warm. Jacoby kept looking at my hair, but he didn't say anything about it. I felt like a bad mother for putting him through so much. It wasn't until I reflected on all that we'd been through these last few months when I realized how much of a burden my marriage had been on our son. First, for Jacoby to learn that Cedric really wasn't his father was enough. Then for him to run around after Cedric's women, asking them to stay out of our lives, that had to be hurtful for him. All he wanted was a stable family, yet what we provided was a dysfunctional mess.

I reached over for his hand and held it with mine. "If Cedric survives this, I don't know where we go from here. But, I want you to let me handle this from now on. I know you feel as if I've been weak, and that's why you've taken things into your own hands. But I got this, trust me. Get back to your life as a teenager and try to have some fun. I don't want you to worry so much about me and Cedric, because—"

"I worry, because no matter what, the two of you are still my parents. I know Cedric isn't my biological father, but he has taken good care of me and you too. He has a high sex drive, and I do believe that your lies contributed to some of this as well. But none of us are perfect, Mama. If I forgive you, I have to forgive him too."

I swallowed and blinked to wash away my tears. "Thank you," was all I could say.

On the inside, I was too angry to forgive Cedric right now. I was too angry about what he had put us through. Yes, he'd provided for his family, but that was what he was supposed to do. I didn't share any more of my thoughts with Jacoby. And as I'd said before, I would handle this.

Jacoby got up to get a soda from the soda machine. He also said he needed to return his girlfriend, Adrianne's, phone call. He walked away to go call her, so I reached for my cell phone to check my messages. I had five messages from Trina. She wanted to know where I was, and she sent several text messages, asking for me to call her back. I really didn't want to be bothered, but I sent her a text, telling her that I was at the hospital waiting to find out Cedric's condition. The second I put the phone back into my pocket, I saw two of the officers from earlier enter through the sliding glass doors. I turned my head, but the one I had spoken to earlier had already spotted me. He wasted no time coming up to me.

"Do you have a few minutes to talk?" he said, scratching his bald head that was full of dents.

I sighed and got up from the chair. Before walking away, I looked around for Jacoby and saw him standing next to the bathroom, talking on his cell phone.

"This will only take a few minutes," the officer said.

I followed him into the hallway, in no mood to be questioned. Didn't they find out everything they needed to know from Rich, Jacoby, and the killer herself? This officer was barking up the wrong tree, and he had racist pig written all over that red, puffy face of his.

I eased my hands into my pockets and leaned against the wall. My blank expression alerted him that I didn't want to be bothered. "What is it that you want to ask me?" I said to the officer.

He pulled out a notepad and scanned his eyes up and down to look at it. "Are you and your husband separated or divorced?"

"Right now, I don't know what we are. But you may want to ask him that question if, or when, he comes out of this."

"I'm asking you. Some of my sources say that the two of you are separated, and that you were angry because your husband filed for a divorce."

My face twisted. "Of course I was angry. But are you implying that I had something to do with what happened?"

"I'm not implying anything. I'm just trying to get to the bottom of this, that's all."

"If you want to get to the bottom of this, go talk to that hoochie who was in the back seat of the police car. She can probably tell you more than I can, and please don't stop there. My husband has been screwing around with several women, so it wouldn't surprise me if they all conspired to do away with him."

"Well, that's why I'm here. Did you pay Paula Daniels to kill your husband? I mean, she doesn't seem like the kind of woman who could pull off something like this alone."

I chuckled and shook my head. "Why couldn't you see her doing it? Because she's a white woman, and they don't do things like that? You would like to believe that I paid her to kill my husband, but if I wanted to do so, you best believe that I would've picked up the doggone gun and shot him myself. You're wasting your time, Officer. Going this route will get you nowhere with me."

He ignored me and kept on with the questions. "Where were you today? Do you have an alibi? And just to let you know, we will be checking your phone records. If there are any conversations between you and Miss Daniels, we'll be in touch."

"I'm not going to answer another question from you. If you want to question me further, you will do so in front of my attorney. Meanwhile, stop showing sympathy for murderers. No matter what color they are, do what you must to keep them behind bars. If not, you're the one who has to live with it, not me. Thank you, Officer. Have a nice day."

I walked away with a mean mug on my face. How dare he go there with me? I figured he wanted someone else to go down for this, other than Miss Prissy whom he obviously felt sorry for. The more I thought about this, the more my anger took over. It got worse when I saw Trina come through the door, searching for me. I cut my eyes and moved in another direction. It wasn't long before she caught up with me down the hallway.

"Stop this, Kayla, and tell me what's going on. Did you attempt to kill Cedric?"

I turned to her and snapped. "Hell, no, I didn't, but I can think of a whole lot of people I wouldn't mind shanking right now. What do you want, Trina? Why do you keep bothering me?"

"If you didn't attempt to kill Cedric then who did?"

"It's none of your business, and if you think I did it then keep on believing that."

"Look, you don't have to get an attitude about it. I asked you that because Jacoby told me you killed him."

"Jacoby was mistaken. Now, tell me again why you're here?"

"I'm here because I'm your friend and you need my support. I get that you're still upset about the conversation that took place at my place earlier, but, at least, now you know the truth."

I pursed my lips and shook my head from side to side. I couldn't help the sarcasm. "Yeah, I do. And I'm so grateful to you for telling me everything. After keeping their little secret and protecting their feelings, thank you, Trina, for all that you've done. As for you being here for me, no, you're here because Keith is still in this hospital from being stabbed by your lover, Lexi. I'm sure you can't wait to get by his side, so don't go pretending to be such a supportive friend of mine, please. I wouldn't call it a friendship, would you?"

Trina narrowed her eyes and muffled her lips. I could tell she was trying to prevent herself from going there with me.

"I saw Keith earlier, so I didn't come back here to be with him. And I'm not going to argue with you about this friendship thingy; been there, done that. When you're ready to talk, call me. I'm here for you, like I've always been. Yes, I've made some mistakes, and I should have told you about Evelyn and Cedric. But I had my reasons for not going there. Reasons that you may or may not understand."

I wasn't the kind of woman to keep up a lot of drama, especially in a public place, but Trina needed to hear me loud and clear. "You mean, reasons that I will never understand. Now, get out of my face, Trina. I'm so done with this right now. You and Evelyn, both, can go to hell."

"I'm too blessed to go there, but do yourself a favor and get a grip. This attitude thing ain't you, and I must say that you don't wear it well. I won't share my reasons for not telling you about your cheating husband and backstabbing friend, but I will tell you this. They have a child on the way, so be prepared for Evelyn to go after Cedric's cash. I don't know if he'll make it or not, but whatever you do, tell her that he's dead. With her believing that he is, that may change the game, if you know what I mean. Meanwhile, I'll keep my distance, yet pray that everything will work out for you."

Trina walked away, leaving me stunned yet again. A baby? It didn't even dawn on me that the baby Evelyn was carrying was Cedric's. I thought it was her ex-boyfriend, Marc's, child. I mean, really? If I'd had a gun, I would have gone back there and made sure Cedric was dead. My anger turned into hate. I just couldn't stay there any longer.

Jacoby was still on his cell phone, talking to Adrianne. When I walked up to him, he told her to hold.

"What did the officer say?" he asked.

"Nothing important. But, uh, if you don't mind, I need to get out of here. I'm not feeling well, and being here is making me sick."

Jacoby frowned. "What about Cedric, Mama? Don't you care about him? Don't you want to know if he'll survive? I know you're upset about all of this, but he's your husband and—"

"And I'm his wife," I shouted. "I am his fuck-ing wife and that bastard cheated on me, got another woman pregnant, and had the audacity to buy another one a house! To hell with Cedric, Jacoby! If you want to stay here, please do. As for me, I'm going home! I need to get the hell out of here and go home!"

Jacoby wiped away sprinkles of my spit that landed on his face. He slowly lifted his phone and told Adrianne he'd call her back. "Then go," he said to me. "Adrianne is on her way up here. I'll call you later to keep you posted on Cedric."

"Don't bother," I said, looking around at the many people staring at me as if I was crazy. It definitely wasn't my intention to put my business out there like this. I was totally embarrassed. "I'm sorry about this, but I . . . I can't do this."

I tearfully walked away and left the hospital. While inside of my car, I rested my forehead on the steering wheel and broke down. Tears wouldn't stop falling. I held my chest, wishing that the pain inside would go away. *Why me?* I thought. *Why did all of this bad news hit me like this in one day?* I felt as if I'd lost everything. Other than Cedric, there was another person to blame. Evelyn. I had to go see her, just to look her in the eyes and give her a piece of my mind.

Almost thirty minutes later, I arrived at Evelyn's loft. Like always, security was walking around, and I saw her car parked in the parking garage. Cedric had probably paid for her car, and I thought about keying the side of it. But after I parked, the security looked at me, smiled, and said hello. I spoke back, but I could tell that he was alarmed by how distraught I appeared. He watched my every move, and unfortunately for me, I wasn't sure if Evelyn would buzz for me to come inside. I took my chances and pushed the code to alert her that someone was there to see her.

Seconds later, her beautiful, blemish-free face appeared on the screen. Why did she have to always look so darn pretty? It wasn't that I was jealous of her, but there was no denying that out of all of us, Evelyn always got the most attention from men. Even while we were in high school, most of the boys wanted to date Evelyn. It could have been because she was a slut, too; a slut who got her hands on my husband, and had the audacity to be pregnant by him.

"Hello, Kayla," she said with that same smug smirk from earlier. "What do you want?"

"We need to finish our conversation. Now that Cedric is dead, I think we should talk about what to do with your baby. You are carrying his baby, aren't you?"

Evelyn didn't say a word. She buzzed me inside, and on my way up in the elevator, I felt as if I wanted to throw up. I swallowed and bit into my trembling bottom lip. When the elevator parted, I looked straight ahead and saw Evelyn standing with the door wide open. Neither of us was smiling and seriousness was locked in our eyes. It was obvious that we were about to handle our business.

I stepped forward, but before Evelyn could say one word, I reached out and slapped her so hard that a new hairstyle formed on her head. My hand stung, and I watched as a red handprint swelled on the side of her cheek. Her forehead lined with wrinkles, and as her mouth dropped open, I turned to walk away.

"Thanks for the conversation," I mumbled. "It was well needed."

"You bitch!" she shouted. "You are going to pay for that! I swear to God that you will pay!"

I ignored her and got back on the elevator. Before it closed, I returned the same smug smirk that she had been representing all day. Whatever she had in store for me, I welcomed it. It couldn't be any worse than what she had already done to me.

Chapter 2

Trina

I was to the point where I'd had enough of Kayla's attitude. Evelyn's backstabbing ways, as well, were too much for me to handle. After Kayla left my apartment earlier to go see about Cedric, I politely asked Evelyn to leave. There were times when I felt as if I had the worst best friends ever. I understood that no one was perfect, but this was too much. I was tired of kissing Kayla's ass, and I always found myself trying to convince her what a good friend I had been. I truly felt as if it wasn't my place to tell her about Cedric and Evelyn, but I decided to poke my nose where it didn't belong and let it all come out today. My timing, however, was off. Evelyn was ready to spill her guts, and Cedric had been shot. Now, here we all were, mad at each other, again, and trying to blame each other for why things had turned out this way.

I waited in my car for a while, and right after I saw Kayla leave the hospital, I went back inside. While speaking to Kayla, I'd seen Jacoby on his cell phone, so I assumed he was still inside. Once I had a chance to speak to him, I was going to spend the night in Keith's room. He was still in the hospital, after being stabbed by Lexi. Thankfully, she was dead, and nobody had to run around searching for the person who was responsible. I was so glad that Keith survived the stabbing incident, and hopefully, Cedric would survive too. No doubt, Kayla was upset right now, but there was no way in hell that she wanted the man she had loved since forever to die.

The moment I entered the hospital, I saw Jacoby sitting in a chair. Another family was gathered in a circle, conversing with a doctor. Seconds later, all hell broke loose. Cries rang out, screams echoed loudly and one lady fell to the floor.

"Noooo," she shouted. "Not my Rico! I can't believe he's gone!"

Several people attempted to help the woman off the floor. She kept kicking and screaming Rico's name. She then grabbed one young man by his shirt and ordered him, as well as several others, to handle the situation.

"I don't care what y'all niggas do," she shouted through gritted teeth. "Y'all find those niggas and do to them what they did to my baby!"

More chaos erupted, especially when one of the family members picked up a chair and threw it. Security was called, and Jacoby and I stepped aside until the chaotic situation cooled down. He told me he still hadn't heard anything about Cedric, so I walked to the check-in station to see what I could find out. The nurse behind the counter looked as if she didn't want to be bothered.

"I know you're busy," I said, deciding to lie about who I was. "But my nephew and I have been waiting for quite some time to see what's going on with my brother, Cedric Thompson. Can you please check with someone to find out?"

"He arrived about forty-five minutes ago, and if the doctor hasn't come out to speak to you, I'm sure it will be soon. As you can see, we've had a lot going on this evening. The night is still young."

To ask for patience, at this time, wasn't understandable. Forty-five minutes or ten minutes, somebody could've come out to say something. For now, our hands were tied so all we could do was wait.

"I'm real worried about my mother," Jacoby said as I sat next to him. "I've never seen her like this. The look in her eyes is cold, and for her to walk out like that was crazy."

"I know, but she's been through a lot these past several months. Give her time, okay?"

"I will. I know how she's feeling, but I feel so bad for Cedric. After seeing him like that, I just can't get the thoughts out of my head. I hope he'll be okay."

"Me too."

Jacoby updated me on what had transpired at Cedric's house. And after he informed me of Cedric's affair with his receptionist, I was numb. No wonder Kayla was so bitter. She definitely had a lot on her plate, and I really wanted to be there for her. I wasn't sure if she was going to head back to my apartment, or if she was going back to the house she once lived in with Cedric. I asked Jacoby to call her, but that was when my cell phone rang. It was Evelyn. I could barely say hello before she started yelling into the phone.

"You'd better get some control over your stupid-ass best friend. Please tell her that if she put her hands on me again, I'm going to press charges and have her arrested."

I rolled my eyes. Some people loved drama and Evelyn was one of those people. "What are you talking about, Evelyn? When did she put her hands on you?"

"She just came over here, claiming that she wanted to talk about the baby. Since Cedric is dead, I figured she would offer me some kind of money to help me take care of our child. I don't know what I'm going to do now, but whatever I decide, please tell her to stop hating because this baby doesn't have anything to do with it."

I wanted to call Evelyn all kinds of names for being so foolish, but I didn't want to waste my time with her. "Can I make a suggestion to you? Do yourself a favor and go see a shrink. If you thought Kayla had any interest in helping you with that baby, you're crazy as hell. I don't know what you're going to do, but please don't count on any funds from her."

"Yeah, whatever. I figured you would take her side, like you always do. Meanwhile, I'm the one over here suffering."

"Girl, bye. I don't know what you consider suffering, but trust me when I say you don't know the meaning."

"How could you say that? I'm pregnant, and now that Cedric is dead, there is no way for me to take care of this baby all by myself. I don't want to have an abortion, but what else am I supposed to do? Kayla's life isn't the only one affected. Just so you know, so is mine."

Thank God the doctor came out and called for us. Otherwise, I was about to let Evelyn have it.

"I gotta go. I'm at the hospital with Keith and he needs me."

"I see who your priority is, so go do you. Tell Keith I said hello, and if his brother, Bryson, is there, tell him I said hello too."

I lied and said I would then ended the call. Jacoby and I rushed up to the doctor who squeezed his eyes and rubbed them before speaking to us.

"For now, he's in serious condition, but stable. He lost a lot of blood, and all we can do is wait. He's a fighter, so I'm hopeful that he'll make it."

I sighed from relief and so did Jacoby. "Ca . . . can I see my father?" he asked. "Just for a little while. I want to see him. Let him know I'm here."

The doctor opened the door for us to come inside. We followed him to a space that was divided by white curtains. "Five or ten minutes," he said to Jacoby. "We want him to rest. It's the best thing for him right now."

Jacoby nodded. We moved behind the curtain and saw Cedric lying there looking casket ready. Tubes were in his nose and mouth. Dried up blood was on his face and hands. The sheets had a few blood stains too, and even though he wasn't dead, he sure did look it. IVs were in his hands and the beeping sound from his heart monitor sounded off. I felt bad for Jacoby who stood there motionless. Hurt was trapped in his eyes, as well as a little fear.

He reached out to touch Cedric's hand, which looked swollen. "Take care, Dad. Just wanted to let you know that I was here. I'll be back tomorrow. Hopefully, Mom will come with me."

To no surprise, Cedric didn't respond. I reached out to give Jacoby a hug, and after ten more minutes, we left. Adrianne was waiting for him in the waiting area. He said that she would drive him home.

"Be careful," I said to them. "Let me know if you speak to your mother. I'll let you know if she calls me."

With a sad look on his face, Jacoby left. I headed to Keith's room, looking like a bum in a plain gray sweat suit that was kind of dingy. I didn't want him to see me like this, but I had rushed out of the house to see about Kayla. A cap was on my head, covering my short, layered hair that needed perming. The only thing jazzy on me was my gold hoop earrings.

I entered Keith's room and saw him sitting up in bed watching TV. Bryson was there, too. He was talking on his cell phone, but excused himself before leaving the room.

"I thought you were going home," Keith said with his gown hanging off his broad shoulders. His muscles were exposed, and in a hospital bed or not, my man always looked sexy. "And where is the cake you promised me?"

"I haven't had time to cook anything. Needless to say, this day has been a day from hell."

Keith patted the spot next to him. "Come here. Tell me all about it. Based on our conversation from earlier, when you promised to tell Kayla the truth, I take it things turned ugly."

"More than ugly. Almost deadly."

Keith cocked his head back in shock. I sat next to him on the bed and began to tell him about the drama between me and my BFFs.

Chapter 3

Evelyn

A week had passed, and to no surprise, I hadn't heard from Kayla or Trina. I, at least, thought somebody would call to let me know about Cedric's funeral, but I guess they didn't want his baby's mama, me, showing up and causing a scene. I was livid. Called myself telling Kayla what was up with her no-good man and this was the thanks I got. It wasn't my fault that she had married a man like Cedric, and any woman in her right mind would've hopped in the bed with him and taken his money too. I was in need of cash, and since he'd offered to pay my rent, I couldn't turn him down. And even though I had to give a little something in return, sex wasn't necessarily a bad thing. Not with a man like Cedric anyway, because sex with him was always finger-licking good. That's what I was going to miss, and there was a tiny part of me that missed him already. I wondered who had shot him. Obviously, not Kayla since she was probably too busy running around, looking for sympathy. Trina would surely give it to her. The next time I saw either of them, I was going to let them have it.

For now, I had to make it to my appointment at the abortion clinic. I thought long and hard about this. It was in my best interest to terminate the pregnancy. I could barely take care of myself. Bringing a child into my unstable situation wasn't a good thing. I figured I would have to seek other alternatives regarding my financial situation. Now that Cedric was gone, my well had definitely run dry.

At first, I wasn't nervous about aborting the baby. But, the moment I walked into the waiting area and saw many others, my nerves started to rattle. I wasn't sure why they were there to see the doctor, and I hoped like hell that nobody knew what I was about to do. I wrote my name on a clipboard and then took a seat. Seemed like everybody's eyes, including mine, roamed around the room. There were fake smiles on display, but I gave no expression in return. All I wanted to do was get this over with, but for the next couple of hours, all I did was sit, think, and wait.

Being there made me think about my parents, particularly my mother. She was so excited about sharing her second pregnancy with my dad, but he wasn't trying to hear it. The moment she showed him the pregnancy test that displayed a positive sign, he washed the smile right off her face. I remember sitting there, watching his fist pound straight into her stomach. She doubled over and fell to the floor. He began kicking her like he was punting a football in the NFL. Told her that she needed to get an abortion, or else he would beat the baby out of her. I wasn't sure what my mother decided to do, but whatever it was, there was no baby.

Dad got what he wanted and his abuse continued. My mother and I, both, caught hell. I despised her for allowing him to get away with so much, and I promised myself that I would never be like her. She lived broke and died broke. Her entire life revolved around my father, and neither one of them gave two cents about me.

The bubbly nurse interrupted my thoughts when she called my name. I followed her to a room where I went through a short counseling session and then I had an ultrasound. An hour later, I was being comforted by a doctor who handled my procedure then wished me well. I was asked to chill in a waiting area for at least an hour, but when no one was paying attention, I slipped out the door and left.

I had never experienced anything so gut wrenching. What I had done to my baby weighed heavily on my mind, but it was my choice—a choice that I had a feeling I would one day regret. I knew I would, especially since I had always wanted a child. Not now, though; when things were in order, when I was married to the man of my dreams, or when I knew that my child's father was capable of being there and providing for our child in a major way. Regardless, I figured that Cedric wouldn't turn his back on me or our baby. He wasn't that kind of man, but a dead man he was.

I was starting to feel depressed so I needed someone to talk to. I couldn't stop crying, and as I looked in the mirror at my puffy, red eyes, I felt shameful. I moved my long hair away from my face and tucked part of it behind my ears. I pictured my beautiful baby who probably would've looked just like me. No question, Cedric was a handsome man too, but my family had strong genes. I rolled my eyes at myself then flushed the toilet and washed my hands. My cell phone was on the counter, so I picked it up to call Trina.

"Hello," she said then laughed. It was a good thing to know that one of us was having fun.

"What's so funny?" I asked.

"Nothing. I was just laughing at something Keith said."

"Oh, I see. So, I guess you're with Keith. Is he out of the hospital or are you at his place?"

"Yes, he's out of the hospital, and I am at his place. Why are you asking?"

"Because I want to see you, spend some time with you. I haven't heard from you, and I'm a little disappointed that you kicked me to the curb because of Kayla."

"I haven't kicked you to the curb. And as a matter of fact, I haven't heard from Kayla. I'm giving the two of you time to chill out and get y'all selves together."

"I can't believe that you haven't spoken to her. I'm sure you went to Cedric's funeral, and I know you spoke to her then."

Trina paused for a while, and then she changed the subject. "What do you want to do? Meet me somewhere for drinks or have dinner tomorrow?"

"I'd rather not go out. Can you come over here today?"

"Not right now I can't. I'm getting ready to start cooking dinner for Keith. We have plans this evening."

"Well, put your sexual plans on hold. I'm coming over there, if that's okay. I promise not to stay long, but I really need for you to lend me your ear. I'm going through something right now, and I'm not sure about what direction I should go. So needless to say, bestie, I need your advice."

"Since when? I doubt that you will listen to any advice that I offer. Besides, Keith has only been home for a few days. We need some time alone."

I winced and rolled my eyes. "This is a life-or-death situation. I'll be there within the hour. Save some dinner for me, and if you're cooking chicken, like you always do, make mine extra crispy. I'm on my way."

I ended the call, and when Trina called back, I didn't bother to answer. Instead, I brushed my hair into a sleek, bouncing ponytail that showed my round face. I put on some ice-blue eye shadow and thickened my lashes with mascara. I added shine to my lips with a clear gloss and sprayed a few dashes of perfume over my clothes. The simple jeans and T-shirt that I previously had on wasn't suitable enough, so I changed into a gray stretch dress that hugged my curves. It was strapless and showed a healthy portion of my cleavage. I accessorized the dress with silver hoop earrings, and the five-inch heels I wore gave me much height. I was sure Trina wouldn't want her best friend looking like a bum around her man, but then again, he was probably used to her sporting sweat suits, jogging pants, and plain ol' T-shirts and jeans all the time. Now that she wasn't claiming her dyke status anymore, I hoped she jazzed herself up and tried to dress better.

I tucked my clutch purse underneath my arm and put on my game face, pretending as if today had never happened. I was so good at hiding my pain, and had learned to do so when my father chastised me about being such a wimp and a crybaby. *Nobody cares about crybabies, and most men won't give a damn about your tears,* he'd say. *Keep it moving and never let anyone see how hurt you really are.* That was what I did when he beat me and had sex with me, too. Pretended as if I wasn't hurt, when deep down I was.

I washed away my thoughts and headed to my car. It was a little chilly outside, but I didn't want to cover up and hide my sexiness. Maybe I'd go somewhere for a drink tonight and find me another rich man who could assist me in my time of need. That was definitely an option, because I was so sure that I didn't want to stay cooped up with Trina's boring self all night.

I stopped at the grocery store, and then arrived at Keith's house almost an hour later. I had never been there before, but awhile back Trina told me where he lived. I was impressed by the humongous, historic house that looked fit for a king. Trina said Keith was just an artist, but I didn't know that artists were doing it like this. I rang the doorbell and could see Trina making her way to the door, through beveled, thick glass. As expected, she had on a pair of navy jogging pants and a half shirt that showed her midriff and tattoo that was drawn near her side. While she was definitely a shapely woman, her muscles always irritated me. I didn't think a woman should look so toned, but that was her preference, not mine. She opened the door, and the first thing she did was look at the card, balloon, and bottle of wine in my hand.

"Really?" she said. "Are you serious?"

"About what?"

"What's with the card, balloon, and wine, Evelyn?"

"The card and balloon is for Keith, and the wine is for dinner. What is wrong with me trying to do something nice?"

Trina removed the card from my hand, but she popped the balloon and left it on the porch.

"That doesn't need to come in here."

I was a little pissed, but I didn't want to argue with her about her jealous ways. She opened the door wider for me to come inside. I looked up at the high, cathedral ceiling and at the wooden staircase that traveled several floors up.

"Wow," I said with wide eyes. "This is nice. No wonder you're over here all the time. It sure as heck is a major step up from your tiny, junky apartment."

"Maybe so, but my apartment is much bigger, better, and cleaner than your loft is. It doesn't surprise me that you're impressed by Keith's house, especially coming from where you just came from."

I threw my hand back, ignoring Trina's comment. Besides, by the way she looked me over, I could tell her attitude was because she was jealous. I watched as she opened the envelope and pulled out the card. I tried to snatch it, but she pulled it away and started to read it.

"'Hope you're feeling better and welcome home. Trina will definitely take good care of you, but if she doesn't, be sure to let me know so I can hurt her.'" Trina pursed her lips and ripped the card in two. "You can be sure that I will take good care of him. This is going overboard, don't you think?"

"No, I don't, but I understand how insecure some women can be at times. It was simply a nice gesture. Nothing more, nothing less."

"I'm sure you said the same thing to Kayla about Cedric. But on another note, thanks for the wine. Dinner is almost done. I hope you can't stay long, and before we go to the kitchen, would you mind telling me why you're here again?"

I released a deep sigh and folded my arms. "Stop being so bitter and just enjoy my company. There was a time when we used to have so much fun. I would certainly like for our friendship to get back to what it used to be, but that's up to you. In addition to that, I had an abortion today. I've been feeling kind of bad and lonely. Wanted to spend some time with my best friend. Is there any harm in that?"

Trina hesitated before saying anything. I could tell that she wanted to reach out to me, but she held back. "I'm sorry to hear about the abortion. Even though I wish you wouldn't have gone there, I respect your decision. Now, do me a favor. Let's not talk about your situation with Kayla and Cedric tonight. I'm so done with that. Have a piece of chicken, drink a little wine, and then get your tail out of here so I can make love to my man. It's been awhile, so you can understand how hungry I am."

Trina laughed and so did I. "Then get your horny self in the kitchen and finish up. And where's Keith? I must tell him how much trouble you really are. Obviously, he doesn't know better yet."

I followed Trina, and when I made it to the kitchen, I damn near stumbled in the doorway. Keith sat at the table with his shirt off and many colorful tattoos were on display. His skin was a dark, luscious chocolate and was shiny and smooth. There was a small bandage at his midsection; I assumed that was where he had been stabbed. His fade was lined to perfection, and the second his eyes locked on me, I felt a trickle in my panties. I wasn't sure if it was blood from the abortion or a gathering buildup from me feeling excited. Keith was almost identical to his brother, Bryson. It was a tossup on who actually looked the best. I mean, I loved the look of Keith's numerous tattoos, but if Bryson didn't have as many, he would be voted the best looking in my book. Maybe one day I'd get a chance to see them both naked. Then I'd be able to confirm either way.

"Evelyn brought us some wine," Trina said, showing the bottle to Keith. He stood and a warming smile washed across his face. His teeth were straight, white, and perfect. I was a little jealous that my best friend had a man like this in her possession.

Keith thanked me for the wine. He moved at a slow place toward me, and then reached out to give me a hug. I purposely pressed my breasts against his muscular chest and held on to the embrace for as long as Trina would allow it. I could see her eyeing me from the corner of her eye.

"You're so welcome," I said. "I also brought you a ca—"

Trina cleared her throat. "Go ahead and have a seat. And I told you I didn't need a *can* of veggies, because I like mine fresh. Keith and I go to the Soulard Market every weekend to get fresh vegetables, don't we, baby?"

"Yeah, we do," he said.

He walked back over to the chair and stretched before sitting down. I couldn't help but to notice his sexiness in the black jogging pants he wore that tied at his perfect waistline. There was also a bulge in his pants. I wondered if his goodness was on the rise, due to our close embrace.

After Keith sat, so did I. Trina stood close by the stove. She was mashing some potatoes while frying chicken at the same time.

"This is almost done," she said. "Evelyn, if you would like to make a quick salad, I'd appreciate it. The lettuce, tomatoes, ham, and eggs are in the fridge. I boiled the eggs earlier. All you have to do is chop them."

"I didn't come over here to cook or prepare anything, but since I'm sure Keith is hungry, and so am I, then I'm going to put the salad together without complaining."

"Well, thank you," Trina said with sarcasm. "Besides, I want to keep you busy while you're here, just so you don't find yourself in that trouble you mentioned earlier."

I laughed and ignored Trina's remark. Truthfully, I could've found myself in trouble. Then again, so could Keith. He kept looking at me, and when I flaunted myself to the refrigerator to get the items for the salad, his eyes were all over me. I purposely dropped a tomato, just so I could bend over. I wanted him to get a clear view of what I looked like in that position.

"I'll be right back," Keith said. "I need to go make a phone call."

"Okay," Trina said. "Take your time. By the time you get finished, dinner should be good and ready."

Trina didn't lie. Within fifteen minutes, Keith returned to the kitchen. The table was set for three, and I took the honor of pouring the wine.

"Half glass or full?" I said while standing in front of Keith with a flute glass in my hand.

"Full," he said. "All the way to the rim."

"All you have to do is ask."

I filled his glass then sat it on the table in front of him. I figured Trina would only want her glass filled halfway, so I poured the wine and placed the glass in front of her. Before pouring my glass, I sat at the table and crossed my legs. I lifted my glass and toasted to good friends.

"May we all stay this close for many years to come."

Trina displayed a fake smile and Keith nodded. Minutes later, we tore into the food and kicked up a conversation that went on for quite some time. Trina directed more of her conversation to Keith, and truthfully, so did I. We talked about his career, his family . . . more so about his brother. Keith definitely had my attention when we discussed Bryson, so I elaborated more.

"Where did you say he worked?" I asked.

"I didn't, but he's a construction manager. The last two projects he worked on were the Stan Musial Bridge and Ball Park Village."

"I bet that was interesting. I have yet to drive across that bridge, but I have been to Ball Park Village. It's nice. Is he married? I saw him at the hospital when you were there, but I didn't get a chance to introduce myself."

Trina and Keith spoke at the same time: "Yes/no, he is/isn't married."

I laughed when Keith looked at Trina who insisted that Bryson was married.

"I'm sure Keith knows if his brother is married or not," I said to Trina.

She gave him an evil gaze, but smiled to play it off. "You're right," she said. "He's not married, but he's engaged, isn't he?"

Keith shrugged. "If you want to call it that, yes, he's been engaged for almost four years. I'm not quite sure if he's found exactly who or what he's looking for yet."

"I know," I said then took a bite of the chicken. "Many of us are still looking for the right one. It's hard to know exactly what you want, and we fool ourselves so many times, thinking and believ-ing that we've found our soul mates."

"I truly believe that I have," Keith said, looking at Trina. "Make no mistake about it, I'm not confused in any way."

Trina smiled then leaned over to give Keith a kiss. I wanted to puke. He only said that because he knew she was pissed about something. Probably about how much he kept staring at me. To me, his eyes said it all. If I wanted him, I could have him. But for now, he had to say kind words to warm her little heart. Too bad he may soon break it.

"Awww," I said with a fake smile. "Isn't that so sweet? I'm glad you're not confused, because Trina was confused for a real long time. When she told me that she was down with women, instead of men, I was like, girl, please. Don't even come to me with that mess. I didn't believe she was trying to go there, but I guess she had an urge. I was totally shocked about the Lexi thing, and I'm sorry you got caught in the middle. I told Trina to always be honest about her feelings. If not, somebody was liable to get hurt."

Trina's face fell flat. I guess my little comment caught her off guard. She lowered her fork to the plate and killed me a thousand and one times with the look in her eyes.

"Just so you know, Keith knows that I used to date women. He knows all about my past relationship with Lexi, may she rest in peace. I don't recall you ever telling me to be honest about my feelings for anyone, especially since honesty isn't exactly your specialty."

I dabbed my lips with a napkin and remained calm as ever. Besides, I was sure Keith didn't want a loudmouth ghetto girl, and Trina was definitely representing.

"I don't know why you're raising your voice. All I did was express to Keith how confused you were about relationships. I've been confused before too, so it's really no big deal. I applaud him, especially if he knows what he wants. Most men don't, but I appreciate those who do."

Keith spoke up before Trina did. "I get what you're saying, and after our little incident, we have agreed to always be open and honest with each other. I doubt that Trina is confused by who she wants, and there was a legitimate reason why she felt a need to pursue relationships with women, rather than men."

"Well, she never shared that tad bit of information with me. And as long as the two of you are happy, that's all that matters. I'm good, but I could be so much better if you'd do me a favor and introduce me to your brother. If he's still confused, maybe I can help him settle his needs and desires, once and for all."

Keith looked at his watch. "Funny you should ask. I told him to drop by after work. He should be here shortly, and you two can have another opportunity to meet then."

"No," Trina said. "I mean, it's not right to introduce him to someone when he's already engaged to someone else. In addition to that, Evelyn is getting ready to go. I'm sure she didn't intend to stay this long."

Trina shot me a dirty gaze and tried to cover it up with a smile. I smiled back, but made it clear that I had nothing else to do.

"I didn't intend to stay this long, but what the hell? And as for Bryson being engaged, allow him to tell me his relationship status. Then we'll decide where to go from there. Who knows? He may not even like me. I might not be his type, so just relax."

"Oh, you're definitely his type," Keith quickly said. "No question about that."

"What is that supposed to mean?" Trina hissed. "Why would Evelyn be his type?"

Keith had put his foot in his mouth without even knowing it. Trina stared at him, awaiting an answer. So did I.

"What I mean is she seems nice. He appreciates nice women with pretty smiles."

His punk ass just lost a few points with me. If anything, he should've been honest and told Trina exactly why he thought Bryson would be interested. It was because I was sexy as hell, way more beautiful than Trina could ever be, and my personality was off the chain. I couldn't even count how many times I'd made Keith smile and laugh tonight. He knew that I was capable of bringing more excitement to his brother's life. Maybe to his too.

"Nice, huh," Trina said then turned to look at me. "Well, I hope your pretty smile gets you exactly what you want."

I displayed that smile she was referring to. "It always does."

Keith sensed an argument brewing so he quickly intervened. "Ladies, I didn't mean any harm. I meant nothing by stressing my brother's taste in women. Ultimately, he'll decide what to do with Evelyn, not me."

Trina didn't appreciate his words. She got up from the table with an attitude. "I'm going to do the dishes. After I'm done, I'm going to bed."

Keith got up and wrapped his arms around Trina as she faced the sink. "You want me to help? How about you wash and I dry?"

"No, I don't want you on your feet for that long. If Bryson is going to be here soon, why don't you go chill in the living room? Turn the TV on, and I'll bring in some more wine before going to bed."

"Are you sure?" Keith said. "I don't mind helping you clean up. I'm not that tired."

"I'm sure. If anything, Evelyn can help me then she can leave. Like I said, I'm a little tired and the bed is calling me."

I guess that was a hint, but whatever. Keith kissed her cheek, and when the doorbell rang, he gave her a light pat on the ass and walked away. She smiled, but I caught her rolling her eyes at me again.

Since I had just gotten my nails done, I wasn't about to help her with the dishes. I stood next to her with my arms folded. "You know, I really don't get why you're being so mean to me. One minute we're cool, and the next minute you're treating me like you don't want to be bothered."

"That's because I don't want to be bothered, Evelyn. You tend to say the wrong things sometimes, and the last thing I needed was for you to remind Keith about why he was stabbed. I already feel bad about the shit. I don't need you up in here talking about how confused I was."

"You act as if being confused is such a bad thing. I meant no harm by my comment, and excuse me if I rubbed you the wrong way."

"Well, you did. Now on another note, you need to forget about pursuing Bryson. From what Keith told me, he has enough drama with his girlfriend. I don't want you to involve yourself in anymore mess, so that's why I spoke up about it."

"Thanks for the warning, but I think I can handle Bryson."

"Just like you handled Cedric, right?"

"I didn't handle Cedric. Obviously, someone else did and good for her. He deserved whatever he got. Remind me to go put some flowers on his gravesite, whenever it dries. I'd hate to get mud on my shoes."

"Well, breaking news. You may want to sit down before I say this to you, but don't go buying flowers just yet. The woman you're speaking about didn't do a good job. Cedric is alive and well. Jacoby told me that he got out of the hospital yesterday and he's at home with his family."

I wanted to punch Trina in her face for lying to me. All she was doing was trying to upset me, because she was mad about the attention Keith had shown me tonight.

"Stop your lies, Trina. Kayla already told me he was dead and so did you. Did he come back from the grave?"

"We both were sadly mistaken. He's alive. Maybe not as alive and well as he could be, but I assure you that Cedric Thompson is alive. I don't mean any harm by saying this, but you should have waited before having that abortion."

The wicked smile on Trina's face cut me like a knife. I felt a hard jab in my stomach that was tied in a knot.

"Don't lie to me, Trina. This is nothing to play with. Is he really alive or is he dead?"

"Why don't you call his cell phone and see? Maybe he'll answer, maybe he won't. If he does, tell him I said I hope he feels better. I'm sure you'll stop by with some wine, a balloon, and a card. If you're planning on giving him a card, make sure you let me sign it."

I wasn't sure if Trina was messing with me. But just to be sure, I rushed to my purse to retrieve my cell phone. I dialed Cedric's cell phone number, and after three rings, a woman answered. I didn't recognize her voice, but I was sure that it wasn't Kayla's.

"May I speak to Cedric Thompson?" I said.

"Mr. Thompson is not accepting phone calls at this time. Would you like to leave a message for him?"

"You said that he's not accepting phone calls at this time. When will he be able to accept them?"

"As soon as he's better, ma'am. I can give him your message, and I'm sure he'll return it as soon as he's able to."

It still wasn't clear to me that Cedric was alive. "What I'm asking is, if I leave him a message, will he be able to get it? I thought Mr. Thompson was deceased."

"No, ma'am. He's alive. You can leave a message—"

I pushed the end button and stood with a stoned face. I could hear Trina whistling in the background. She had the audacity to giggle.

"Told you so," she teased. "Now, getting back to that card. Are you going to go purchase it, or shall I?"

I swallowed the oversized lump in my throat and tucked my purse underneath my arm. I was in no mood to entertain Bryson now, but the second I entered the living room, there was hope. Needless to say, Bryson was one fine motherfucker. I felt another trickle, especially when he stood and extended his hand to me.

"I'm Bryson, Keith's brother. I believe we met before, at the hospital. I can never forget a face as pretty as that one."

I was deeply hurt inside about Cedric being alive, but I couldn't help but smile at Bryson's kind words, as he towered over my short frame.

"Yes, I remember seeing you at the hospital. It is such a pleasure to see you again."

"Why don't you have a seat and join us for some drinks? I haven't had dinner yet, so maybe Trina can whip me up a plate and bring it to me."

Bryson looked over my shoulder at Trina. She winked at him and promised to bring his plate in a minute. Meanwhile, she stepped up to me and whispered in my ear.

"Whatever you do, don't turn around. Take what's in my hand, go to the bathroom, say good-bye, and then leave."

I wasn't sure what the hell Trina was up to. Whatever it was, I backed out of the living room and removed what was in her hand. When I looked at it, it was a maxi pad.

"You're bleeding," she said. "See, if I was a dirty friend, I would have let you flaunt yourself around, like you've been doing all night, and embarrass yourself. The least you can do is thank me. Your abrupt departure will let Bryson know you're not interested, unless you want to go back in there with that stain on the back of your dress."

I was floored. Without saying another word, I rushed to the bathroom to check my blood flow. Trina was right. I would've embarrassed myself big time. I was seconds away from turning around so Bryson could get a glimpse at my shapely behind. I hurried to clean up, and before I made a swift exit, I poked my head through the living room's wide doorway.

"Fellas, I'm sorry. I have an emergency, so I have to leave. Bryson, I hope to see you soon, and Keith thanks for letting me stay for dinner. Take care, okay?"

They looked confused. Bryson stood and offered to walk me to my car.

"No, please, I'm good," I said. "Stay. I promise you that we'll speak soon."

Trina rushed me to the door and I didn't say another word to the men. While on the porch, I whispered for her not to tell Keith about my little incident.

"Good-bye, Evelyn. Go home and see about yourself. And leave Cedric alone. Let that man rest and wash your hands to that situation."

I didn't reply. Trina knew I wasn't about to make that kind of promise.

Chapter 4

Kayla

The good thing was that Paula Daniels was behind bars. She confessed to trying to murder Cedric, and the focus had been taken off of me. Jacoby was delighted that Cedric was recovering well, but the unfortunate thing was that I wasn't.

I wanted to forgive Cedric for all that he'd done, but I couldn't. I couldn't find the right time to speak to him about his affair with Evelyn, and now that he was home, I didn't want to be in his presence. So instead of staying in the house, I moved my things out of Trina's apartment and went back to a hotel room. This time, I had money in my pocket, and I withdrew a substantial amount of money from Cedric's bank account; money that could assist me, until I decided what to ultimately do. The divorce papers that he'd sent to me, right before he was shot, awaited my signature. I wasn't sure

if I would sign them, but for now, the papers
sat on the table in the hotel room, along with
several checks that I'd written to take care of
his bills, along with mine. With Cedric unable
to handle things, I took the initiative to make
sure everything was taken care of. He was very
organized, and as I searched his office, I found
a list of his monthly expenses that needed to be
taken care of. I also found a list of the numerous
payments he transferred to Evelyn's account,
and additional payments he sent to other wom-
en's accounts as well. I didn't know who any of
the women were and some of the deposits into
their accounts could have been work related.

The house that his receptionist lived in had
Cedric's name on it. After he kicked her out,
he'd planned on renting the place. At $5,000 a
month, it was obvious that she hadn't been living
in a shack. Evelyn was the one who had gotten
duped. Her loft was nice, but in no way could
it have been like the house Paula had lived in.
Speaking of being duped, that applied to me too.
There were hotel receipts from when Cedric was
out of town. He paid for dinners, plays, cars, and
then some. He damn sure wasn't cheap when it
came to giving money to his mistresses, but they
all were required to put up with his mess. What I
discovered was there were plenty of women who

seemed willing and able: willing to hurt me and destroy our family, like Cedric was.

Since Jacoby decided to stay at the house with Cedric, I felt a little better. I didn't want Cedric being alone, so what I did was hire a maid/nurse's aid, Cynthia, who was capable of taking care of him. Ever since he'd been home, I stopped by to check on him. Some days he didn't know I was there, other days he would see me but wouldn't say much. According to Jacoby, he said he and Cedric were starting to talk more. He said they had a few positive conversations, and Jacoby had asked me when I was coming back home. At this time, I wasn't sure.

I entered Cedric's house through the front door. Jacoby was sitting on the couch in the great room, watching TV with Adrianne. They both smiled when they saw me.

"Hey, Mama," Jacoby said, standing up.

So did Adrianne. She reached out to give me a hug. "Hello, Mrs. Thompson. How are you?"

"I'm doing okay. What are you all watching on TV?"

"ESPN," she said then playfully rolled her eyes. "We're going to the movies in a little bit. Would you like to go with us?"

"No, not today. Maybe some other time, but thanks for asking."

Cynthia came into the room to join us. She wiped her hand on an apron and nudged her head toward the kitchen. "May I speak to you for a minute, Kayla?" she said.

"Sure." I followed her into the kitchen, where she was preparing a meal. Whatever she had in the oven smelled delicious. I could tell it was something sweet. I'd definitely try whatever it was, especially since I'd lost so much weight in the past few months. My curves were starting to disappear and this was the smallest I'd been since college.

Much shorter than I was and a bit on the chubby side, Cynthia stood in front of me. She gave me a piece of paper and showed me Cedric's phone. "This woman called four times for Cedric. She didn't want to leave a message, but she sent a text telling him to call her, once he was better. I just thought you may want to know this. Also, another woman left a message for him. It was very sexual, and I assume she doesn't know what happened."

I took the phone, and sure enough, one of the numbers belonged to Evelyn. I guess she must have figured out that Cedric wasn't really dead. I thanked Cynthia for the information.

"No problem. Mr. Thompson has been asleep for most of the day, but the last time I checked on him, he was up watching television. I think he's starting to feel better, because I heard him laugh when speaking to Jacoby. You have a very loving son, but sometimes he walks around here in a daze. I ask if he's okay, and he says that he's fine. I think this whole thing with his dad is kind of troubling him. But it's good that he's been here for his dad. They seem to like each other's company, and all in all, you do have a good son. Your husband, however, is a little demanding. But that's okay. I know how to deal with him, and when I offer him my fist, he laughs."

"Thank you for the information, Cynthia. I think Jacoby will be fine, and he is a good kid. I wouldn't have him any other way. As for my husband, good luck with him. That's why I'm paying you extra, because I know he's a force to be reckoned with."

We laughed and Cynthia agreed.

"Now, what's for dinner?" I asked. "If you made some more of that delicious lasagna you made the other day, I'm staying."

She lifted her finger and switched it from side to side. "Listen, girlfriend, I may be an Italian woman, but I also like to experiment with soul food. I'm cooking a delicious pot roast, mac and cheese, candied yams, and greens. My cherry cobbler is in the oven, and I can't wait for you to taste that."

"I think you may have to leave the soul food to me, but we'll see. Let me go talk to Cedric. The conversation that I have with him will determine if I'll stay."

I walked past the great room where Adrianne and Jacoby seemed to be enjoying each other's company. As I slowly made my way up the stairs, I stopped to take a deep breath. I wasn't prepared to look face to face with Cedric since he'd been shot and today was no different. But after I paused, I continued up the stairs and into the bedroom. I was pleased to see him lying on his side, sound asleep. The TV was on, and I turned to see who the person was on TV yelling. It was a commentator on ESPN, talking about sports. I couldn't believe that his foolishness had caught my attention. So much so that when Cedric called my name, I barely heard him.

"Kayla," he called again. I turned and saw him adjusting himself to sit up in bed. "Do you mind helping me with a few of these pillows? Bring me some of those pillows at the bottom of the bed so I can prop myself up."

Just because I didn't want to come off as bitter, I did what he'd asked. I fluffed the pillows and placed them behind him. He appeared comfortable and smiled. "Thank you. And if you would please get me a glass of water, I would appreciate it. I think Cynthia has an ice bucket over there. My glass is right here on the nightstand."

I didn't budge. I folded my arms and stared at him. "I don't mean to be rude, but let me say this to you. I am not starring in a role for *Diary of a Mad Black Woman,* so, therefore, you won't find me around here washing your tail, cooking and cleaning, feeding you or massaging your back for you. It pains me to fluff your pillows and get you a glass of water, simply because I don't appreciate all that you've done to me. I don't have to recall everything you did, but just so you know, the baby is a hard pill for me to swallow, Cedric. So was the affair with your receptionist, and let's not talk about all of the others. I'm here to make sure you're being taken care of by Cynthia. Also to see about my son, and to make sure the bills don't get behind. If there is anything pertaining to the bills that you would like for me to take care of, please let me know."

Cedric let out a dry cough and then he wiped his mouth. He reached for his glass on the nightstand and reached out to hand it to me. "My mouth is dry. There is ice in the ice bucket and water in the bathroom. Would you please take care of that for me?"

I stood my ground. "No. I will let Cynthia know what you need, and since you're paying her well,

I'm sure she will abide. Now, if there is nothing else pertaining to your finances, I'm going to go."

Cedric didn't say anything else, so I moved toward the door. When he called out my name, I halted my steps.

"There is one thing," he said then lightly chuckled. "No, two. Be sure to put aside some money to buy my baby some Pampers when he or she arrives, and buy yourself a wig, too. Your short haircut looks as bad as that attitude you got, and don't come here again until you figure out how to sympathize with me regarding this situation. Yes, I created a mess, but don't you stand there being all innocent and shit, like you're so gotdamn perfect."

This bastard had my blood boiling. Yet again, I was the one to blame for his fuckups. I wasn't sure when he was going to fess up and take responsibility for what he'd done. I already admitted to how hurtful my lies about Arnez being Jacoby's father may have been, but I wasn't going to take the blame for anything else. I marched over to the bed and poked at his wounded chest. He squeezed his eyes, revealing that he was in a little pain.

"Buy your own baby Pampers, and you can keep on paying for all of those hoochies' pussies too. I have lost all respect for you, Cedric. A huge part of me wish . . . I wish you would've died!" I choked back my tears, realizing how difficult it was for me to say that to him.

He appeared stunned too, and this time around, his voice softened. "Don't worry about my finances. All I want you to do is sign those divorce papers and free yourself. After you do that, I assure you that you'll feel a whole lot better. Now leave so I can get some rest. I've had enough arguments with you. Quite frankly, they're not worth my time."

I took a hard swallow and tried to gather myself to say something else to him that would hurt. Instead, I stormed toward the door and slammed it behind me. When I reached the bottom stair, I looked into the great room at Jacoby and Adrianne.

"Tell Cynthia I'm not staying for dinner. I hope the two of you have a great time at the movies. When you get home tonight, Jacoby, please call me."

"Will do, Mama. Holla tonight."

I left, feeling on edge. Every time Cedric brought up those damn divorce papers, it upset me. Every time I saw him, I wanted to scream at the top of my lungs and punch him a thousand and one times. But the truth was, for me to allow him to upset me like this, it proved that I still loved him. There was something inside of me that didn't want to let him go. I didn't want any of those other women to have him either, and I hated myself for still having feelings for him—no, for loving him. The hold he'd had on me needed a retirement date. I needed to retire him, but unfortunately, I didn't know how long his hold would last.

I was so wound up that, almost an hour later, I found myself following Evelyn as she made her way to the grocery store. She parked and hopped out of her car as if the paparazzi were waiting to snap a picture of her. She removed her shades and tossed her long hair from side to side. She was so busy trying to make sure everyone noticed her that she didn't even see me coming up from behind her. I tapped her shoulder. She swung around and frowned at my presence. Catching her off guard, again, I slapped the mess out of her.

"I'm not going to keep having these conversations with you," I said, pointing my finger near her face. "Stop calling my husband and leave us the hell alone."

I walked off, but this time, Evelyn came after me. I'd known her for many years, so I already knew that she didn't know how to fight. She was too worried about not looking cute, but that was the least of my worries.

"Your ass is going to jail," she shouted then slapped her hand against my back. "You're not going to keep slapping me and getting away with it!"

I turned around and grabbed her neck. I squeezed it as hard as I could, causing her to weaken and almost melt close to the ground. She squeezed her eyes and scratched at my hands so I would loosen my grip. I did and that was when she grabbed her own neck and rubbed it. She was doubled over, trying her best to catch her breath.

"I swear." She kept choking. "Yo . . . you are so in trouble. I am pressing charges today!"

"Do what you wish. Besides, I have money for a lawyer; how about you? Probably not, and trust me when I say it will be your word against mine. But if you want to resolve this little matter, and stop having these abrupt conversations, then leave me and my family the hell alone. The choice is yours."

People going into the grocery store had stopped to look. But no one was about to interfere when it came to two black women going at it. I saw one lady reach for her cell phone, so I pushed Evelyn one last time. She stumbled, but managed to stay on her feet. I walked to my car and listened to her numerous threats. All they did, for the time being, was make me laugh. I felt as if I'd gotten some kind of satisfaction.

Chapter 5

Trina

Maybe it was just me blowing things out of proportion, but Keith had me a little hot the other night when Evelyn stopped by. All of a sudden he seemed to perk up, and every time she got up from the table, I saw him gaze at her ass. I saw his eyes drop to her cleavage, and his comment about Bryson's taste in women rubbed me the wrong way. And then to imply that Bryson would be interested because of her smile, that was an insult to my intelligence. Really? That's the real reason I was mad, in addition to Evelyn's snide remarks.

Then again, like I'd said, maybe I was tripping. Evelyn was a nice-looking woman. What man wouldn't give her a double look? There was a time when I had her on my to-do list too, so I guess I could give Keith a pass. That night, however, I didn't give him a pass. I went to bed, while he and Bryson stayed up playing cards. They invited two more of their friends over, and by the time they all left, it was almost four in the morning. Keith came to bed that night, drunk and looking for some action. I was in no mood, and as horny as I was, I had to diss him for giving Evelyn too much attention.

I had been spending so much time at Keith's house that my poor little apartment was being neglected. Kayla had removed the majority of her things, and it had been a few weeks since I'd last heard from her. I wondered how she was, especially since Evelyn had called to tell me about another incident between them at the grocery store. I told Evelyn that I didn't want anything to do with what was going on between her and Kayla. I also reminded her that calling Cedric wasn't the brightest thing to do. She accused me of making her reach out to him, but it was the only way she would believe that he was alive. I figured she regretted the abortion, even though she hadn't yet admitted it.

For the next few hours, I stayed home and cleaned up. My apartment was a mess. Kayla didn't help me clean up while she was living here, and it was apparent that she was used to a maid cleaning up the big house she lived in with Cedric. I mopped the floors, washed the dishes, and took out the trash. I also cleaned the bathrooms, but as soon as I plopped down on the couch to rest, Keith called.

"Are you coming back over tonight?" he asked.

"Not tonight. I've been cleaning up all day, and I'm kind of tired. I'll stop by tomorrow. I'm going to the grocery store first, so let me know if you need for me to pick up anything for you."

His masculine, sexy voice transmitted through the phone and right into my ear. "All I want is my woman and some juicy oranges. A loaf of raisin bread would be good, too, but nothing would satisfy me more than being with my lady right now."

I took that as a hint that Keith didn't want to be alone tonight. He definitely knew how to put a smile on my face. He also knew how to get me to change my mind.

"How badly do you want to see your woman? She's tired, lazy, and a little groggy. She may not be good company tonight, but after she gets her beauty rest, she will feel so much better."

"Truthfully, I love her even more when she's tired, lazy, and a little groggy. Can't be up all the time, and trust me when I say I can handle it. Besides, the last time I checked, she rests pretty well when she's with me. Right in my arms and sleeping like a newborn baby."

I couldn't deny that. So instead of staying home, I told Keith that I would stop by the grocery store then come to his house.

Within the hour, I was at his place. Two bags of groceries were in my hand, and I unlocked the door with the key he'd given me. The downstairs lighting was dim, but when I looked up the staircase, I saw a light on in his bedroom. I could also see a sliver of light coming from the kitchen, so I made my way to it to put up the few groceries I'd had. As soon as I reached the kitchen's doorway, Keith startled me and crept up from behind. He slipped his arm around my waist and unhooked the button on my jeans. A burning candle was on the kitchen table, along with two plates topped with Chinese food that smelled pretty darn good.

"Since our dinner was ruined the other night, I thought I'd make it up to you. But first, you got to do a little making up yourself, if you know what I mean."

I dropped the bags on the floor and stood as Keith unbuttoned my jeans and pulled them down to my ankles. As I stepped out of them, he lifted my tank shirt over my head, and in one snap, he unhooked my bra. I stood in my yellow lace panties and could feel his naked body pressing against mine. When I tried to turn around and face him, he wouldn't let me.

"I need to work it out from back here, first. Then we'll seek another position."

While still in the doorway, Keith remained behind me. He massaged my tiny breasts together and placed a trail of delicate kisses along the side of my neck. My head was tilted and eyes were closed. I felt so lucky to be with him, and shame on me for acting so foolish the other night.

"Mmmm," Keith moaned while playfully biting my neck. "You smell like Pine-Sol."

I opened my eyes and couldn't help but to laugh. "I told you I'd been cleaning up. You wouldn't let me do anything else, but rush over here to see you."

"That's because I had something to give you. And as soon as you remove those panties, I'ma show you exactly what it is. I'm also going to be generous and let you feel it."

I lifted my arms and placed my hands on the back of Keith's head to rub it. "I like it so much better when you remove my panties. For some reason, when you do, my pussy tends to perform better."

Keith massaged my tight abs, twirled his finger around in my belly button then lowered his hand to cuff my pussy. He pulled the crotch section to my panties aside and pushed two of his thick fingers into my heated pocket. Almost immediately, I straddled my legs and ground my hips, as if his fingers were his dick easing in and out of me. He made it feel that way, and my wetness caused a heavy buildup of cream on his fingers. I was so wet, but there was something in his touch that always brought out the best in me.

Aside from our moans, we could also hear my juices being stirred. Keith added another finger, and he worked them inside of me so well that I was now on the tips of my curled toes. I pushed my ass in his direction, and I could feel his hardness fighting back. It grew against the crack of my ass, and the more I felt his growth, the more I wanted him inside of me. I yanked his fingers from my insides, lowered my soaking wet panties, and hurried toward the kitchen table. While bending over, I reached back to spread my ass cheeks apart. My moist hole smiled at Keith, who in return, stepped forward and positioned his dick to enter me. He loved to tease me, but I was in no mood for foreplay.

"Put it in there," I whined. "I want all of it, baby. Drive it all the way up in there."

"As wet as you are, I may skid on the icy road and hurt myself. Something tells me that I'd better take it easy or else."

"Yeah, well, something tells me that if you don't stop teasing me like this, you will hurt yourself. I won't take it easy on you, so you'd better take advantage of working this out from behind."

"I love tough talk, baby. Bring it on."

Keith assisted me in holding my ass cheeks apart, and then he plowed his dick far inside of me. He rocked me at a swift pace from behind, so fast that I had to reach out and hold on to the table. I felt every single inch of him gliding in and out of me, and the sounds of my pussy gushing echoed in the room. I did my best to keep up with Keith. Every time I pushed back, he answered with a long stroke that caused my legs to weaken.

"I know you ain't going to sleep on me, are you?" he said, holding my waist to keep me on my feet.

"Noooo," I cried out. "It's just that . . . that your dick feels so good that I'm melting. I can't help it that I'm weakening and melting like this."

Keith snickered. I had to admit that it was pretty funny too, but it was the truth. I was melting right in his hands, and when the tip of his head shaved against my clitoris, it was all over with for me. I damn near fell to my knees. The orgasm I had was that damn good. Keith had to pick up my trembling body from the floor. He carried me upstairs to the bedroom and laid me back on the bed. I had finally calmed down. That was when he lay over me and wrapped my legs around his back.

"I say to hell with dinner," he suggested. "Let's finish what we started, and this time, I want you to hurt me like you said you would."

I wasn't sure if I had enough energy to *hurt* him or not, but I rolled on top and gave it everything that I had. Even that didn't seem like enough, but whether it was or not, we spent the next couple of hours making love. Afterward, I fell asleep in Keith's arms. Just as he had predicted, I slept like a newborn baby.

By morning, I rolled over and yawned. I looked for Keith, but he wasn't in bed. I was naked and my body was sore all over. I also had a headache, so I sat up and massaged my forehead. Wanting to take a shower, I got out of bed and grabbed towels from the closet. I then looked in the medicine cabinet for aspirin, but there were none. I did, however, see two boxes of opened condoms. From both packages, one condom was missing. I thought that was kind of odd, especially since I felt as if we had developed a trusting relationship and had stopped using them. I provided the ones we had used in the beginning of our relationship, so there was no way for him to say that he'd used the condoms with me.

I closed the medicine cabinet and laid the towels on the counter. Not sure where my clothes were, I looked into his closet to get one of his T-shirts. It barely covered my ass, but for now it had to do. I walked down the stairs and could hear rap music coming from the kitchen. When I entered, Keith was standing by the stove, flipping pancakes. My eyes scanned down his backside that was without a stitch of clothing. Sexy, he was, but not sexy enough for me to forget about the condoms.

"Since we skipped dinner," I said, getting his attention, "I guess we're now on for breakfast."

Keith turned around and smiled. He licked his lips then wiped his mouth. "I don't know about you, but I ate pretty good last night. Got full, too, and it's been a long time since I felt that fulfilled."

"A long time as in maybe three weeks? We did indulge ourselves, right before . . . never mind."

I hated to talk about the incident with Lexi. It made me revisit how wrong I was for lying to her, and for almost causing Keith to lose his life.

"It's okay to talk about what Lexi did. I'm over it, trust me. I hope you are too."

"It may take me a little longer than you to get over it, simply because I don't like the fact that you got hurt."

"So did you. But there's no need for us to harp on the past. I'm all about the future, so I have a question for you. Come closer so I can ask you this."

I walked farther into the kitchen and stood by Keith. He lifted a fork and picked up a slice of his pancake. "Open your mouth and tell me how that taste. To me, it tastes rubbery. But maybe it's just me."

I laughed, thinking that he was about to ask me something else, like if I would marry him. Lord knows I wasn't ready for that. Even though I loved Keith, I still believed that even our relationship was young. Maybe after another five years, I'd be ready to walk down the aisle.

I opened my mouth and he put the pancake inside of it. It didn't taste rubbery to me. Actually, it tasted pretty good.

"You're good," I said with a nod. "Throw in two sausages, a slice of bacon, and some orange juice and you'll be on point."

Keith grabbed my waist and positioned me to face him. We shared a lengthy kiss then he spoke up again. "You know that's not really what I was going to ask you, right?"

"No, I didn't know, but spill it. What's on your mind?"

"I want you to move in with me. I miss you when you're not here, and I hate calling you all the time, begging and pleading for you to come over."

He was teasing me about the begging and pleading part, but he seemed serious about me moving in with him.

"I'm not so sure if I want to do that just yet. Give me some time to think about it, and I'll let you know, okay?"

Keith held a blank expression on his face. He didn't appear to like my answer. He let me go and turned to face the stove. He flipped another pancake and placed another one on a plate. "What's there to think about?" he said. "And why wouldn't you want to move in with me?"

"For starters, I don't want to rush into anything. Sometimes, I need my space and I assume that you do too. I also question if you're seeing somebody else, especially since you have open boxes of condoms in your medicine cabinet."

Keith's head snapped to the side. His brows curved inward and he cocked his head back. "Condoms? Yes, I do have open boxes of condoms, but in case you forgot, we used to use them."

"You're right, we did. But I was the one who always had them, not you. Not once did you ever use any of your condoms."

He quickly shot my comment down. "That's a lie. I know what I used and who I used them with. And for you to suggest that I've used them with someone else is stupid. As it is for you to question if I've been seeing someone else, when you know damn well that the only person I've been with is you."

"So, in other words, you just called me stupid? If I'm so stupid, then why do you want me to move in with you? That's stupid for you to ask, especially if you think I'm so stupid."

Keith turned to me with much frustration on his face. "You know what's stupid? This conversation. Obviously, you woke up on the wrong side of the bed. I don't have time to argue with you this morning, and forget about me asking you to move in with me. I shouldn't have ever asked."

"No, you shouldn't have, especially since you can't figure out why you have two open boxes of condoms. When you figure that out, maybe we can talk about moving in together."

I cut my eyes at him and walked away.

"Not interested," he said underneath his breath. "Silly shit, I swear."

I turned around and put my hand on my hip. "Silly? Now I'm stupid and silly. Wow, Keith. It's great to know how you really feel."

He laid the spatula on the stove then faced me. "You want to know how I really feel? I'll tell you how I feel. I feel as if, for some reason, you are holding back on this relationship. That makes me uneasy. You purposely came down here this morning to start an argument with me; that way you can go home and get some of the so-called space you need. I don't know what's preventing you from giving me your all, but maybe like Evelyn said the other night, you're still confused. If you are, just let me know. That way, I don't put my all into this relationship and wind up hurting myself again. Been there, done that before. Ain't trying to go there again, so your honesty about how you feel, as well as about how confused you may really be, would be much appreciated."

Did he seriously just go there and bring up Evelyn? No, he didn't. "I'm not holding back on anything. Just because I don't want to move in with you right now, it has nothing to do with me being confused. The problem is you not getting your way. You can't accept no, and that's all there is to it. I didn't purposely pick an argument with you. You're the one with condoms that aren't accounted for, so don't go turning this around like I don't have my head on straight. In addition to that, if you think Evelyn has a valid point, then why don't you call her up to chat? I'm sure you would like that, especially since you couldn't keep your eyes off of her the other night."

Keith nodded and sucked his teeth. "Okay, I finally get it. That's what this is all about. You've been holding that shit in since the other night. I'm glad you got that off your chest, and just so you know, Trina, I can look all I want to. It's a good thing that you never know what I'm thinking, as I am doing right now while looking at you. Lastly, I can accept no, if you say it. Now that you've said it about moving in together, I accept it. Forget it and let's move the hell on."

I wasn't sure how to take his comment, but more than anything, the thought of him thinking anything about Evelyn upset me. I rushed up to him, ready to smack some sense into him. But before I got within inches of him, he stepped back.

"Think before you act," he said. "I don't fight women, and if you ever put your hands on me in an offensive way, this shit is over. If I want a ghetto girl, I'll go get one."

"I'm sure if you want one with a pretty smile, you'll go get her too. I'm out of here, Keith. And save those rubbery pancakes and your condoms for the next woman you want to trick."

Keith walked around me and went to the closet. He removed my jeans and T-shirt from inside, and then made his way to the door. After opening it, he made a gesture with his hand.

"Get your clothes on and go. There are plenty of men who may want to spend their time arguing with you and dealing with your insecurities. Unfortunately for you, I'm not the one."

I continued to rant and change my clothes right at the door. And as soon as I stepped outside, Keith slammed the door behind me. It was a good thing that he'd shown his true colors before I decided to move in with him. I hurried to my car, thinking how badly he had screwed himself. I also wondered if I had done the same.

Chapter 6

Evelyn

To be honest, things were getting a little bit rough around here. Now that I no longer had Cedric to depend on for money, everything was behind. I had been on two job interviews, but neither of them panned out for me. One only paid eight dollars an hour, and the other one was too far away. The manager who interviewed me had nothing but jealously in her eyes, so I suspected that she wouldn't offer me the job anyway.

When I returned home, there was a note from the rental office on my door. I was almost two months behind on rent. The landlord gave me until the end of the week to come up with at least one payment. Not to mention that my car payment, light bill, and personal property taxes were due. I was now driving around with improper plates, and it was just a matter of time before the police would pull me over and give me a ticket.

The only thing that I could do, for now, was gather up some of my expensive clothes and purses that Cedric had given me money to buy, and see if I could sell them to a consignment shop. There was one in Ladue. From what I'd heard, they paid a nice piece of change for brand name clothes and purses. I piled the items into my car and headed to the consignment shop to see what I could get. I had so many items bunched in my hand, and when I placed them on the counter, the lady behind it looked at me like I was crazy.

"How may I help you?" she said in a snobby tone.

"I want to see what I can get for these items."

She lowered her glasses and winced at the items. "Are they real or knockoffs?"

I didn't want to insult this bitch, but she sure did insult me. Why would I even come here, if my items were knockoffs? I placed my hand on my hip, and rolled my neck around. "Where do you get off asking me if they're real? Do I look like I wear knockoffs? I think you'd better look again, because I only wear the real deal, sweetie. Thank you very much."

The old, angry-looking white woman sorted through the items, laying them flat on the counter. She kept looking at the labels. When it came to the purses, she kept looking inside and feeling the leather.

"I'm not sure about this one," she said, referring to my Michael Kors bag. I used the money Cedric had given me to purchase that one at Macy's.

"If you're not sure, then you need to question Macy's about selling counterfeit purses. I assure you that they're not getting their purses from Soho in New York."

"Maybe not, but since I'm not sure about that one, I can't give you a quote on it. As for the other items, how much do you want for them?"

I was desperate for money, so I didn't want to get on this bitch's bad side and argue with her about the purse. Instead, I quoted her on what I thought the ten items were worth.

"How about five . . . no, six thousand dollars?"

Finally, the lady laughed and removed her glasses. "That's funny," she said. "And now that you're done joking with me, how about telling me how much you really want for these items?"

I looked at her with a straight face. "I just told you how much I want, and since I'm not smiling, you know I'm not joking. In case you're not bright enough to know what these pieces are worth, please check the price tag on the one right there. I've never worn it, and it cost twelve hundred dollars. The others I may have worn once or twice and they cost the same, maybe even higher. I'm sure you already know how much the purses cost, and three of them should tally up to what I want. Got it?"

The woman was blunt. "What you want, you won't get here. Got it? This is a consignment shop, where our customers expect to pay a discount for brand name merchandise. The clothes are wrinkled, and I won't mention the stain I see on one of the dresses. Looks like the same stain Monica Lewinsky had on her dress, but I'm not one to assume anything. As for the purses, they are not in tiptop condition. The most I could give you for all of this is five hundred dollars. That's it."

I couldn't hold back, especially not after the Monica Lewinsky comment. "Bitch, are you crazy? Five hundred dollars? I should jump over this counter and knock some sense into you. At that price, you shouldn't be working here. You apparently don't know the value of these items. And stain or not, you know darn well that this stuff is worth way more than that. I could go stand on a corner and sell these items for more than that."

"Then I suggest you go do that because all I can offer you is five hundred dollars. Since you don't want to accept my offer, good-bye and thanks for stopping by."

How dare this snobby heifer treat me like this? I snatched up my items and stormed out of there. I tossed the items on the back seat and slammed the door after I got inside. My mind was racing a mile a minute. I couldn't think of anywhere else to get some quick money, other than to rob a bank. I had to laugh at how desperate I'd become, and the thought of robbing a bank was a bit much.

I started my car and breezed my Mercedes with improper plates on it through traffic on Lindbergh Boulevard. Just as I was about to get on the highway, my cell phone rang. I looked to see who it was, and surprisingly, it was Trina. I hadn't spoken to her since the other night, but I had planned on calling her so I could get Bryson's number to call him.

"Hello, bestie," I said in a joking manner. "It's good to know that I'm on your mind, or should I say your radar today."

"I'm not going to say all of that, but I called so we could talk. Keith and I had an argument, and I wanted to ask if you thought I was wrong about something."

This was interesting. Trina and Keith always seemed so chummy with each other. And while many couples had arguments, Keith didn't seem like the arguing type. As for Trina, that was a different story. She could be a real shit starter, if she wanted to be. I'd known that from experience.

"What happened? Tell me."

Trina told me about the condoms and about him telling her to leave. I wanted to laugh my ass off. I envisioned his foot traveling deep in her ass when he kicked her out. Either way, I gave my input to my friend who seemed distraught about what had happened.

"First of all, you had every right to be mad," I said. "I would have questioned those condoms too. At the end of the day, he needs to provide you with a legitimate explanation for the ones missing. He didn't have an answer; that's why he kicked you out and made you leave. He's hoping that you forget all about it, and that you'll miss him so much and come running back to him. If I were you, I wouldn't. I'd keep it moving and find someone else who has no problems with being honest."

Trina sniffed then blew her nose. "I agree. He made me look like the bad person, and then had the nerve to say that I was stupid and silly. That hurt. I never thought Keith would speak to me like that."

"I don't know why you thought he was so special. He's just like any other man, and to be honest, the last thing you need is another mentally abusive man in your life. The last one you had was both physically and mentally abusive, and you see where that got you. With that crazy bitch, Lexi. You definitely don't want to go there again."

"No, I don't. I don't get why relationships are so hard, but maybe it's time for me to step back and chill for a while. I need to get myself together before I start dating again."

"I agree. I feel the same way. I have so much going on right now that I can't even think straight. My bills are way behind, and I've been on four or five interviews. The job market sucks. I haven't found anything yet."

"Eventually, you will. And if you need to borrow a couple of dollars, let me know. I could spare twenty or forty dollars, but that's it."

I pursed my lips. What in the hell was I supposed to do with twenty or forty dollars? That was barely enough for me to get my nails and toes done.

"No, thanks, I'm good. At least until I get my unemployment check, so no worries. In the meantime, you need to chill and forget about Keith. I'm out and about right now, so if you want some company, let me know. I'll stop by to chat."

"I'm leaving in a few to go to the studio and get some work done. Whenever I'm this upset, I like to paint. You'd be surprised by what I come up with, when I'm feeling down like this. Painting always makes me feel better."

"Well, go do you. I'll call to check on you tomorrow."

"Thanks, Evelyn. I really do appreciate it. I know we've had our ups and downs, but at least we can still have a decent conversation with each other."

"You're right. I've known you since elementary school, and we've had way more ups than downs. You'll be okay. I'm sure that I will be too. By the way, have you heard from your attack dog, Kayla?"

"Don't say that about her. And no, I haven't heard from her. I've thought about calling her, but since I've been in touch with Jacoby, he says that she's doing okay. I'm giving her time to sort things out. She has a lot on her plate with Cedric. I assume that she doesn't want to be bothered."

"We all have a lot going on, but you already know how Kayla is. Her problems are always bigger than everyone else, and we're supposed to stop what we're doing to see about her. I haven't talked to her since the incident at the grocery store. I guess she hasn't been in the mood for another one of her so-called conversations that consists of her slapping me."

"No comment. I'm not touching that thing with you and Kayla. Maybe one day y'all will work it out."

"I doubt it. It doesn't matter to me either way, but I'm going to let you get out of there and go to the studio. Have fun and remember what I said to you about Keith. A dog will be a dog, and sometimes, you have to let him bark and dig his own grave."

Trina said good-bye. I hoped she had washed her hands of Keith, but I knew how my BFF's were. They didn't always want to walk away from relationships, even when they knew they should have.

I drove to my next destination, which was only five minutes away. That would be Keith's house. I hoped he was home.

I parked my car and strutted to the door. After ringing the doorbell, I waited for him to answer. Minutes later, I saw him coming down the stairs. He appeared upbeat and was dressed in a pair of white cargo shorts that were unzipped and hung low on his waist. They looked dynamite against his chocolate skin, but unfortunately for me, he had on a wife beater that covered up part of his chest. Still, the man was sexy as ever. *Trina had better get herself together—fast.* No man wanted to be involved with a woman who kept up a lot of foolishness. She whined too much, and he couldn't be happy about her appearance that didn't seem to be her priority. She never wore name brand anything. The least she could do was carry a name brand purse. Every real woman had at least one.

Keith swung the door open with a grin on his face. "What's up, Evelyn? Trina's not here. If you need to reach her, you may want to hit her up on her cell phone."

"Oh, I know she's not here. She told me earlier about the brutal argument the two of you had. Since I was in the neighborhood, I wanted to stop by to see if I could convince you to give me your brother's telephone number? The other day, Trina didn't seem as though she wanted me to have it. I don't know what's been up with her attitude, and I don't appreciate her being all up in my business. She's been acting real funny lately. I think it may have something to do with . . . never mind. Forget it."

As I predicted, Keith opened the door wider for me to come inside. He wanted to know what was really going on with Trina. I would happily fill him in.

"You don't have to stand out there. Come in."

"Are you sure?" I said already stepping inside. "I mean, you weren't busy, were you?"

"I was upstairs in my studio, painting. Whenever I have a lot on my mind, it's usually what I do."

Awww, they were like two peas in a pod. Trina had just said the same thing; they clearly had something in common.

"Your studio? You have a studio in here?"

"Yep. On the third level. Would you like to see it?"

See that and then some, I thought. "Yes, I would. Trina told me what a great artist you are. I thought the two of you worked together; and didn't you meet her at that, uh, studio on Delmar?"

"Yes, I did. I haven't been there in a while, though, but I may stop by next week to attend an art show."

I wanted to yawn. How boring. I focused on something other than his conversation, as he made his way up the stairs in front of me. His nail-gripping ass was right there, waiting on me to touch it. All I wanted to do was reach out and touch it, but Trina would kill me. I had a vision of his muscular body on top of mine, sweating while we fucked each other's brains out. I would put any amount of money on it that Trina didn't know how to utilize a man like this. Keeping him excited would be difficult for her. That was why he needed me.

By the time we made it to the third level, I was out of breath. I stood in the doorway, watching as Keith proudly showed me some of his paintings. There was no question that the man had talent. His studio had some of the most exquisite pieces of art I'd ever seen. I was in awe as I looked around the room. The smell of money was floating in the air and these pictures had to be worth a lot of money.

"Oh, my God," I said, walking up to a colorful painted picture of Miles Davis. "This is so beautiful. A friend of mine would love this! Miles is his favorite jazz player. I have never seen anything like this before."

"I sold the original to a museum in Atlanta. Unfortunately, that one there isn't for sale."

"I'm not trying to be nosy or anything like that, but how much does something like this cost? You have so many beautiful pieces in here. I wonder how much they're worth."

Keith shrugged and boasted about his work that was quite impressive. "Anywhere from five to thirty or forty thousand dollars. It depends on what I'm asked to do. I have some wealthy clients who pay high dollars for their artwork. They often refer me to others, so I stay quite busy."

"I see," I said, gazing around at the large room. "And it's a good thing that you love what you do. I wish I could discover what my real talents are. Maybe I would be able to make money like this, but for now, it is what it is."

Keith sat on a stool next to his work station. He invited me to have a seat on the couch in front of him. I did and crossed my legs.

"So, what is it that you exactly do, Evelyn?"

I didn't appreciate him getting all up in my business, but if we were going to get to know each other on another level, why not?

"Currently, I'm unemployed. I was working customer service, but I got laid off. I've been looking for work, but it's hard to find a job. Many economists claim the economy is recovering, but I'm not feeling it yet. My bills are behind, and everybody I try to borrow money from is in the same predicament."

"Yeah, that's too bad. But keep your head up, though. Things will get better."

I was sure that he would offer me a little something, but at least he gave me hope. He started to dabble on a sketchpad that was on his workstation. I admired a man who utilized his talents to make money; and, all the way around, he was so damn gorgeous to me.

"While at the door, you mentioned something about Trina's strange behavior," he said. "Do you mind elaborating on that?"

Keith's eyes scanned my moisturized legs, which were still crossed. Then his eyes traveled from my head to toe, before he looked at the sketchpad again and waited for me to reply.

"What I meant by that was I told Trina she needed to knock it off. No offense to her, but there are times when she chooses to be a drama queen for no reason. It irritates the heck out of me, and I reminded her that no man would put up with that mess. We had a little argument because she didn't like what I had to say to her. Please don't tell her that I'm sharing this with you, but she be acting a little off at times. I told her that she needs to go get herself checked out, and that's why I said she was confused the other night. She is confused. When I say that to her, she takes it personal."

Without looking up, Keith hit me with more questions. "Confused about what? What do you think she's confused about?"

"Honestly, I think she's confused about being with you."

He finally looked up and wet his lips with his tongue. "Why would she be confused about being with me?"

"I say that because when we talk about y'all's relationship, she always hesitates and brings up her past. She talks about her attraction to other women, and I'm not sure if she's satisfied with being with a man. I could be wrong. Trina is very hard to read, but she's been that way for a very long time."

Keith sat quietly for a while. I could tell he was in deep thought. His pencil scribbled faster and the frown on his face said that he wasn't too pleased. I wanted to turn his frown into a smile.

"What are you doing over there?" I asked.

"You'll see. In a few more minutes, you'll see."

Keith continued to dabble while I turned my head to look around the room. I noticed a beautiful painting of Aretha Franklin, but as I scooted forward to get off the couch, he stopped me.

"Don't move just yet. Give me about ten more minutes."

I smiled, figuring that he was creating a sketch of me. "Work your magic," I said. "Had I known that you were creating a sketch of me, I would have gotten myself in a better position."

"The one you're in right now is just fine."

I relaxed back on the couch and spread my arms on top of it. "Okay, if you say so. Have at it, if you will."

Almost ten minutes later, Keith turned the sketchpad around, showing me the picture he'd drawn. I was floored. It was the most awesome drawing of a person I'd ever seen. My mouth was wide open. I peeled myself off the couch and walked up to him.

"Tha . . . that is magnificent. You're so talented, Keith. How did you do that so fast? I kept moving around, talking; you make it look so easy."

Keith was all smiles. The way to any man's heart was to compliment his work. "It was easy, especially when I'm working on someone like you."

I cocked my head back in surprise. "What is that supposed to mean? Someone like me who—"

"Someone like you who is very attractive and funny. That's why I think you'll be great for my brother."

Now was the perfect time for me to make my move. I was close to him, and his masculine cologne drew me right in. I didn't want to let his compliment with regard to me go to waste. I placed my arm on his shoulder and gazed at the sketch in his hand.

"Yeah, I could be great for your brother, but something tells me that I could also be perfect for you too. I don't know why, but I have a feeling inside of me that says so."

Before Keith responded, I removed the sketch from his hand and placed it on his workstation. I stood in front of him and my other arm rested on his shoulder. The direction of my eyes traveled to his thick lips, but as I inched forward, he backed his head away from me.

"Uh, I don't think this is a good idea."

"I'm on the other side of the fence. I think it's a great idea."

I leaned in again. This time, my lips touched Keith's. I forced my tongue into his mouth, and as soon as I felt his, he jumped up from the chair.

"I think you need to go," he said.

I glanced at his hardness that was showing through his shorts. "You're doing a whole lot of thinking, Keith, but your thoughts are not beneficial to either of us. This time, I won't push. You know where I stand, and if you're ever in need of a real woman, who knows exactly what she wants, call me. If you decide not to, I will settle for your brother. Give my number to him, and we can go from there."

I picked up the sketch pencil and scribbled my number on the drawing he'd created of me.

Keith stood in silence as I said good-bye and
sauntered my way toward the door to exit. I
walked down the stairs, and with a smile on
my face, I opened the front door and headed
to my car. Twenty minutes later, I stopped at
a gas station to get gas and a lottery ticket.
Rubbed the ticket and won $500. Somebody
was definitely looking out for me, even more so
when my cell phone rang and it was Bryson. No
question about it, this was my lucky day.

Chapter 7

Kayla

I was sitting in the hotel lobby, having a few drinks at the bar and listening to a man playing some soothing music on a piano. The past few days had been peaceful, especially since I hadn't stopped by the house to see Cedric. Jacoby met me for dinner last night and he updated me on what had been going on at the house. According to him, Cynthia had been taking very good care of them, and Cedric was starting to move around. Jacoby asked me to free my mind of all the hatred I had inside of me. He stressed that if he could move on, I should be able to as well. He had no clue that I still loved his father. That was why I chose to minimize my visits. The last thing I needed was for Cedric to manipulate me again. If I continued to show up and show concern for him, he'd do just that. I felt like such an idiot for not putting closure to this yet, but I guess that timing was everything.

Later that night, I returned to my room. The first thing I looked at was the divorce papers that were still sprawled out on the table. I had picked them up a million and one times. Read them over, time and time again. Cedric didn't agree to give me half, but what he offered was a measly 20 percent for all of the headaches and setbacks he'd caused me. 20 percent was all that I was worth to him, not to mention that he'd get to keep the house. I basically had to start all over and make it work with 20 lousy percent.

Thinking about it, I tossed back another drink. The vodka burned my throat, but it relaxed me. Relaxed me so much that I fell back on the bed and started to laugh at this situation, instead of crying about it. This was it, the end, and it was time for me to get on with my life. I rushed up from the bed and straightened the pile of papers on the desk. I tucked them inside of my purse and snatched my keys off the dresser. I tossed back one more shot of vodka, and then stumbled to the door and left.

Feeling woozy, I plopped down in the driver's seat of my car and revved up the engine. The clock showed one minute after midnight, but I didn't care. I needed to sign these darn papers and deliver them to Cedric ASAP. Should have done this a long time ago, but today felt like the day that it needed to be done.

I swerved in and out of traffic, occasionally crossing the yellow and white lines. My eyes fluttered and felt real heavy. I didn't think I was that drunk, until I heard a loud horn that caused my eyes to shoot wide open. The man next to me lowered his window.

"Watch where the fuck you're going, you dizzy broad! You almost hit my freaking brand new car!"

I lifted my middle finger. "To hell with your car! I hope you have insurance!"

He shook his head and sped off in his Corvette. Who was he to say something to me, when he was driving that fast? I did slow down, but this time I was moving too slow. Other drivers blew their horns as well, yelling for me to get off the road. I honored their requests, just for a little while. My first stop was at Evelyn's place. Luckily for me, I didn't have to buzz for her to let me in. A resident and his girlfriend were going up on the elevator. I leaned against the wall, trying to rest my body that felt limp.

"Are you okay?" the man asked with his arm around his girlfriend's shoulder.

"Yeah," the woman said. "You don't look so good."

I threw my hand back at them. My voice slurred a little. "No, trust me, I'm fine. It's been a long day. I juss . . . just wanted to stop by to see an old friend of mine."

They didn't respond. Got off the elevator at the fourth floor, while I made my way up to Evelyn's loft. I straightened my jacket and patted my hair. The stylist trimmed it for me earlier, and no matter what Cedric said, I thought it looked pretty darn good. My pants didn't hug my thighs like they used to, and in less than a week, I was down another three pounds. Barely able to stand, and wobbling from side to side, I knocked on Evelyn's door. There was no answer, so I knocked harder. This time, I moved closer to look into the peephole. I squinted and blew my breath on the door.

"Trick, I know you're in there. Open the door, so I can tell you how much yo' ass done ruined my life. It's what you want to hear, isn't it?"

Just then, Evelyn snatched the door open. She had on a soft purple robe that cut right at her thighs. Her hair was covered with a scarf and her makeup-free face was blemish free.

"I can't believe this," she said, crossing her arms in front of her. "The perfect princess is at my door, drunk. If you came here to have one of your conversations, I'm not interested. I'm tired and I'm in no mood to keep fighting with you."

I forced myself to stand up straight, as if I had it all together. "That's because you can't fight. Not one lick, and you always needed me to help you when you got beat up by those other kids. I was always there to help you, but you sure as hell didn't help me. What you did was fuck me over and I will nevah, evah forgive you."

"I don't recall ever asking you to, so why don't you take your highly intoxicated ass elsewhere and leave me alone. You told me to stop calling Ceddy, so I did."

I laughed and slapped my leg. "Ceddy? That's my nickname for him, so I wish you wouldn't be a little copycat. But then again, that's what you've always been. Everything I have or have had, you want. You want to be me, Evelyn, but there is only one bad bitch out there who goes by the name of Mrs. Cedric Thompson. Or should I say went by that name because I"—I pointed to my chest—"I'm throwing in the towel. I came to tell you that you and your baby can have him. After today, he's going to be"—I paused and hiccupped—"be a free man. I, on the other hand, will be a free woman with twenty percent of his income."

Evelyn shook her head and gazed at me with disgust. "You're pathetic, Kayla. Truly pathetic.

No wonder Cedric found himself curled up in my bed with me."

I reached out to slap Evelyn, but this time, she grabbed my hand and shoved me backward. I couldn't keep my balance and fell on the floor.

"If you're still out here in one minute, I'm calling security. Cameras are all over the place, and I assure you that, this time, you will be arrested."

Evelyn slammed her door. I barely had enough energy to peel myself off the floor but I managed. I stumbled back to the elevator and held on to the rail as the elevator went down to the parking garage. Somehow, I managed to get back into the car, and I drove myself to Cedric's place. Jacoby's car was parked in the curvy driveway. Adrianne's car was behind his. I wondered what she was doing over here this late; and if I were here, this would never be.

I put the key in the door and pushed it open. It squeaked, but inside of the house, there was nothing but silence. I used the railing to pull myself up the stairs. By the time I reached the second floor, I could see that Jacoby wasn't in his bedroom. Figuring that he was probably downstairs, I headed to the bedroom I once shared with my fake husband. I pushed on the double doors, watching as he lay there sound asleep. It must've been nice that one of us was resting well.

"Yo," I shouted loud enough for him to hear me. "Cedric, get up. I need to get at you 'bout something real important."

I staggered over to the bed. He didn't move, so I leaned down and placed my lips close to his ear.

"Get up!" I shouted. "Don't you hear me?"

Cedric jumped from his sleep and damn near fell out of the bed. He frowned at me and blinked several times to focus.

"What in the fuck are you doing?" he barked.

I put my hand on my hips and pursed my lips. "I . . . I'm doing what yo' grimy tail asked me to do. I'm signing these doggone papers so that we, you and me that is, can be free to fly like little birdies."

I turned in circles, and flapped my arms as if I were flying around the room. Cedric sat up in bed and turned on the lamp. I could see him shaking his head.

"So, here you go." I dug in my purse, trying to retrieve the papers. When I pulled them out, my purse fell on the floor and all of the contents inside scattered on the floor. I dropped to my knees, attempting to stuff my things back into my purse. But when I spotted a pen, I reached for it.

"Ah, ha!" I said with glee in my eyes. I held up the pen, showing it to Cedric. "There it is. Exactly what I was looking for. My little penny pen. Do you see it?"

Cedric didn't say a word. I plopped on the bed and slammed the messy papers on my lap. I scribbled my signature on the long line then tossed the papers at his face. I swiped my hands together then leaned in closer to him.

"Done. All done, and now you can move the hell on. Just make sure I get my twenty freaking percent because I have places to go, people to see, and a new life to go live."

Cedric reached out to grab my face. He held it close to his and our eyes searched into each other's. "I hate to see you like this," he said in a whisper. "No words can express how sorry I truly am, but after all that's happened, I know that saying I'm sorry will never be enough."

"Yeah, well, I . . . I'm sorry 'bout this too, but it is what it is."

I hiccupped again, and before I could back away from Cedric, vomit rushed up my throat. All I remember was it spraying in his face. After that, I blacked out.

I woke up in the morning, not knowing where I was. My head was banging, and the room I was in felt like it was spinning. I yawned and cracked my eyes wider to look next to me. That was when I saw Cedric. He was sitting up in bed with a food tray resting over his lap. A piece of toast was near his mouth and his glass of orange juice wiggled as the bed moved when I tried to sit up.

"Wha . . . How did I get over here?" I asked.

A wet rag dropped from my forehead, and I had on a tacky flowered nightgown that definitely didn't belong to me.

"I can't believe you don't remember."

Cedric seemed to have an attitude, but I was concerned about how I'd gotten there. I remembered driving last night, and I also remembered walking up the stairs. That was pretty much it.

"I don't remember everything, but I guess it doesn't really matter. I do know what I had to drink, and . . . What's that smell? Something smells funny."

"Maybe we didn't get a chance to clean up all of your puke. That could be what you're smelling."

I tossed the covers aside and sat up. "I vomited? Where?"

"All over the place."

"Stop lying, Cedric. You're just trying to make me feel bad."

"If you don't believe me, fine. Go ask Cynthia. I'm sure she'll tell you all about it, especially since she and Jacoby had to help me clean you up."

I got off the bed and looked down at the tacky nightgown again. Maybe that explained why I was wearing it. I left the room, and when I entered the kitchen, Cynthia was making breakfast.

"Good morning, Mrs. Thompson," she said.

"Kayla will suit me just fine, Cynthia. Now please tell me something. What happened last night? How did I get into this gown?"

She smiled at me from behind the island. "Do you really want to know?"

"Yes, I do. Please tell me."

Cynthia told me everything that happened last night. From me throwing up in Cedric's face, to him giving me a shower. She was the one who cleaned up my vomit and changed the sheets. And Jacoby was asked to help carry me to bed, because Cedric was too weak. Now, I felt really embarrassed. I apologized to her, and when I asked where Jacoby was at, she said he had already left with Adrianne. That reminded me about seeing her car parked outside last night, so I excused myself from the kitchen and went into another room to call Jacoby. He answered the phone, appearing to be out of breath.

"Where are you?" I asked.

"I'm at the gym with Adrianne. Are you feeling better?"

"Much better, and I apologize for whatever happened here last night. You already know that I have a lot of things on my mind, and even though alcohol isn't the answer, I used it to cope."

"No need to explain yourself, Mama. I can honestly say that I understand. I'm dealing with some things too, and trust me when I say that you're not by yourself."

His comment caught me a little off guard. I thought things were getting better for Jacoby. Apparently, something else was stressing him. "Do you mind telling me what else you're dealing with? Does it have anything to do with why Adrianne is here in the wee hours of the morning?"

"She's not always there in the wee hours of the morning. Sometimes, but not always."

"Sometimes is more than enough. You know that's something I didn't allow while I was here, and I definitely don't allow it when I'm not. With that being said, answer my question. What else are you dealing with?"

I heard Jacoby sigh. He wasn't trying to have this conversation with me this morning. "Whatever you say, Mama. And the only thing I'm dealing with is school. Can't wait until the semester is over."

"Why? Are your grades suffering? The last time we spoke about school, you said your grades had improved."

"They're up and down. But I'll work it out, like I always do."

"I'll make sure you do, and when I get back to the hotel, I'm going to look at your grades on parent portal. If anything isn't up to par, you know you're going to hear about it."

"I'm sure I will. Meanwhile, I'm trying to get my workout on. Can I hit you back later?"

I wasn't sure if his grades were the issue or not, but I left the conversation there. I told him to enjoy his workout, and asked him to call me later. After I ended the call, I went back into the kitchen where Cynthia was. She interrupted my thoughts.

"Don't look so worried," she said. "I hope you're in the mood for breakfast, because I made enough for everyone. I thought Jacoby and his girlfriend wanted something to eat too. Unfortunately, they didn't."

"All I want is some orange juice and something light, like a bagel. No cream cheese, because my stomach is upset."

Cynthia stopped what she was doing to pour me a glass of orange juice. She got me a bagel from the fridge and brought everything over to the table.

"Tell me something." I looked at Cynthia and thanked her. "How often does Adrianne spend the night? She's not over here during the week, is she?"

Cynthia hesitated to speak. I figured that she didn't want to get Jacoby in trouble, but with her not saying anything, I suspected that Adrianne had been spending plenty of nights here.

"I really don't want to interfere, Mrs. Thomp . . . Kayla, but the truth is, she has been over here quite often. Jacoby has skipped school a few days, too, and I have seen them in some"—she cleared her throat—"questionable positions."

I figured there was more to it, and I didn't know why I had a feeling that Adrianne was pregnant. Jacoby's behavior alerted me that something was really wrong. "Thank you for telling me that. I'll be sure to add a little something extra on your check. Is there anything else I should know?"

Cynthia pulled back a chair and sat down. She clenched her hands together and rubbed them. "No, not really, other than Cedric is getting better. He's been speaking to several people, including a few women who called to check on him. He's been walking around a lot at night, but during the day he uses his cane. I don't think your friend, Evelyn, has reached out to him again. But I haven't looked at his phone in nearly two days."

I placed my hand on top of Cynthia's. "Again, thanks for the update. You have my number, so be sure to call me if you think there is something urgent I need to know."

Cynthia nodded. She told me she had washed my clothes for me and went to the washroom to get them.

I finished my bagel and orange juice then made my way back upstairs with my clothes thrown over my shoulder. When I entered the bedroom, Cedric was now on his laptop, appearing to be occupied.

"Thanks for your assistance last night," I said. "I apologize for throwing up on you. By the way I feel there will be no more drinking for me."

"I doubt that, but if that's how you want to cope with your pain, do whatever you wish."

I ignored Cedric's comment and went into the bathroom to change clothes. I used his wave brush to brush my hair then slipped into my heels, which I saw thrown in the corner. Unfortunately for me, one of the heels was broken.

I held the shoe in my hand and went back into the bedroom. "What happened to my heel?" I asked.

Cedric looked up and shrugged. "That probably happened when you were turning in circles, trying to pretend that you were a bird flying. You stumbled, and I do believe that was when you broke your shoe."

"I think you're exaggerating about some things. Why would I be turning in circles, trying to fly around like a bird?"

"Because you were celebrating. Celebrating this."

Cedric removed a piece of paper from the nightstand and reached out to give it to me. It was the last page of the dissolution of marriage agreement. My signature was poorly scribbled on the line.

"I didn't sign this," I said, handing the paper back to him.

"Yes, you did."

"It doesn't look like my signature."

"But it is. I saw you do it and you used this pen right here." Cedric lifted the pen and showed it to me. "Now, my question to you is if you were serious about it. Are we going to move forward with this divorce?"

"You're asking me as if I have a choice. You're the one who presented me with those papers, so I assume that you still want this to go as planned. Or have things changed?"

Cedric licked his lips then scratched his head. He rubbed the scruffy hair on his chin then shifted his eyes back to me again. "A lot has changed. I don't want the divorce, but I totally understand if you do. So, yes, I'll let you decide what to do. However you want this to pan out, I'll roll with it."

Honestly, I was stunned. It was funny what being so close to death could do to a person. Cedric had a big change of heart.

"Why would you let me decide, especially since you confessed to not loving me anymore? You couldn't stay married to a woman you didn't love; and what about your baby on the way? You know darn well how I feel about that, and we would have a very difficult time, trying to get that to work."

"Yes, we would, but I have a feeling that we would manage. We've been through a lot, Kayla, and I think it may be safe to say that our bad days are finally behind us. As for me not loving you anymore, you know I said that shit to upset you. The truth is, I do still love you. Very much. And I have a feeling that you still love me too."

See, I knew this would happen. Cedric was a master manipulator. He was saying anything right now to get me back on his team. Unfortunately, I felt it working.

I bit my nail and swallowed the lump in my throat. "I've been tricked before, Cedric. And I doubt that a bullet to your chest is going to change anything. You still have a baby to deal with, other women at your beck and call, and Lord knows what else. I don't want to keep going down this road. For you to—"

"I'm a changed man. I don't even believe that Evelyn's baby is mine, and there are no more women. The majority of them all scattered when they thought I was dead. The only person who has been here for me is you. While you haven't been at my beck and call, I know you've been here almost every day to check on me. That means a lot, Kayla, and I'm telling you right now that I want my family back."

This time, I nibbled on my bottom lip. I took another deep breath and narrowed my eyes to look at Cedric. "All we're going to do is argue. You're going to continue disrespecting me and—"

"I only argue and disrespect those who disrespect me. I went there with you because you did the same with me. Like I said, all of that is now in the past. Allow us a new beginning, and if there are some things that you need to get off your chest, do it now. Curse me the fuck out, if it makes you feel good. Slap me, hit me, beat the hell out of me if it helps. Let's get it all over with. Whatever you dish out, I'll take it like a man who wronged his wife. I'm not going to say much more, but once again, the ball is in your court. Take at least another week to think about this, and then let me know. I'm not going anywhere, and as you already know, I'll be right here, waiting."

I stood speechless. I couldn't even look at Cedric much longer, because I didn't want him to sense what I was thinking. A huge part of me wanted to reconcile, but then there was something inside telling me to run like hell. Then, of course, there was this little thing with Evelyn. How I wished I could go tell her that Cedric and I would be together forever. That we survived this setback, and that our marriage was going strong. I wanted to send a message to all of his mistresses, letting them know that they could not tear apart what God had put together. This was my husband, and no matter what, I would be keeping my status. And that included the money. I wouldn't have to start over, and I could kiss that lousy 20 percent good-bye. All of those thoughts swarmed in my head. I was in no position to answer Cedric right now, so I left out of the room without giving him an answer. I told Cynthia good-bye and reminded her to tell Jacoby to call me later. I needed to get him straight again, but not as bad as I needed advice from my BFF. I called Trina to see if we could meet somewhere.

Chapter 8

Trina

I received a call from Evelyn telling me about Kayla showing up at her loft drunk, and then I got a call from Kayla asking if I would meet her for lunch. The one person who I hadn't gotten a phone call from was Keith. I was a little disappointed, too. By now, I thought that he would realize his mistakes and contact me to apologize. I felt as if I had been in the wrong too, and I intended to tell him that, if he called. But the no call meant that he didn't want to reconcile our differences. And if he didn't want to, neither did I.

Kayla wanted to meet at Bar Louie in the Central West End. I arrived a few minutes early, but shortly thereafter, I saw her coming down the street. She looked as if she'd lost a lot of weight. The wide-legged gray pants she wore were hanging on her. Her off-the-shoulder red sweater was pretty, and I loved her short haircut. With her weight disappearing, now she really looked like a runway model. As for me, I sported the usual because I preferred to be comfortable: had on a neon and black sweat suit with Nike tennis shoes. My layered hair was always on point, and my face was makeup free. I didn't get off into all the glam, but both of my best friends did.

Kayla walked into the restaurant and saw me sitting at a table. It had been awhile since we'd seen and or talked to each other. I had to admit that it was like a breath of fresh air to see my friend. I missed her, and by the wide smile on her face, I could tell she missed me too.

She walked up to me and we tightly embraced. Tears welled in my eyes, but I quickly blinked them away. I didn't like to get all emotional, but there were times when I couldn't hold back. We sat across from each other, and I was the first one to speak up.

"First things first," I said. "I don't want any apologies from you, and I will not offer an apology either. What's done is done. Let's focus on the positive, and whatever you do, please don't bring up Evelyn."

Kayla held out her hand and shook mine. "Deal, but you know I gotta talk about Evelyn."

We laughed and hurried to order our drinks and food.

"I'm glad you called me," I said. "I'd been thinking about calling you too, but I wanted to give you some space. If you don't mind me asking, how's Cedric doing? I had been talking to Jacoby for a while, but it seems as if he's been busy. I haven't been able to catch up with him lately."

"Yeah, he's been all right. Busy having sex in Cedric's house since I'm not there. Busy skipping school and spending way too much time with Adrianne."

"Sounds like the typical teenager, but the sex thing is a bit much."

"Yes, it is. As for Cedric, he's doing much better. I haven't officially moved back into the house, but I do stop by to check my boys. I hired a nanny to take care of things for me while I'm away."

"I hope she's not young, sexy, and available. If she was, you know that Cedric would have her in that bedroom and on her back in a minute."

I laughed, but Kayla found no humor in my comment. She stressed that Cynthia was an older Italian woman who wasn't Cedric's type.

"Forgive me for saying that," I said, correcting myself. "I was out of line."

She threw her hand back at me. "Don't worry about it. With his reputation, we all know that anything is possible. But, he has admitted to being a changed man. That's what I want to speak to you about, because I'm so confused. Do you believe people can change? Especially men who have the kind of reputation you mentioned? I don't know what I should do about my marriage. Sometimes I feel as though I want it to work, other days not so much. It's time for me to make a decision."

For the next hour or so, Kayla spilled her guts to me. She laid everything on the line about her feelings for Cedric, about her reasons for wanting to leave, as well as her reasons for wanting to stay. She even told me about how she wanted to slap Evelyn in the face with the news of her and Cedric possibly staying together, but then I decided to hit her with more news.

"She had an abortion. Got rid of the baby the second she thought Cedric was dead. That was why I told you to mention that to her. While I'm sad that she went that route, I figured that it would make things easier for you and Cedric. I really can't say if the two of y'all should work things out or not. That's a tough call, because you know how I feel about him. I'd be wrong to weigh in, but if I must say, I do believe that people can change."

Kayla's eyes looked as if they were about to break from the sockets. "She had an abortion? For real?"

"Yes. She told me that she couldn't afford to raise a child without his support."

Kayla shook her head. "What else did I expect from a woman like Evelyn? If she thought Cedric wasn't going to give her a hard time with that child, she was sadly mistaken. He wasn't even sure if the baby was his. If I didn't see the pregnancy test for myself, I wouldn't have believed her. I don't believe in abortions for any reason at all, but I can't say that I'm not happy about her no longer being pregnant with his child."

"So, does that change things? Does it make your decision to reconcile with him much easier?"

Kayla sighed. "I don't know. Cedric has hurt me so much. I think it would be almost impossible for us to put all of this behind us and carry on as if none of this ever happened. It would take years of counseling for us to get through this. I don't know if I have the time or energy and I don't believe he does either."

"Nothing is impossible. I mean, look at us. Our friendship has endured a lot too, but here we are, sitting here conversing and enjoying each other's company. Never say never, Kayla. You just don't know what the outcome will be."

Kayla agreed with me. The waitress came with more drinks and food, and that was when I started to tell her about my setback with Keith. I wondered if Kayla wouldn't weigh in on my issues with him, since I failed to go there with Cedric.

"I don't want to go there with you, Trina, but what are best friends for, if we can't be honest with each other and speak our mind? So, here it goes. Keith is a very nice man. I'd hate for you to lose him, and maybe, just maybe, you were confused about the condoms. Did you look at the expiration date? They could have been in there for a while. Maybe he forgot about them."

"If he had forgotten about them, he should have said so. And then to kick me out like that and not call me, you know that was foul."

"It was, but some men don't like to argue. He doesn't come off as the arguing type, and look at all of the wonderful things about him. Personally, I think you should call him. It was a petty disagreement that should have never gone this far."

"Evelyn said that I should kick him to the curb. She thinks that he's been lying to me, and to be honest, I'm not so sure about him and his ex. He had some deep feeling for her. I don't think he's quite over her yet."

"Well, Evelyn said that Cedric has the biggest penis ever and she lied. She said that he was in love with her, and she lied about that too. I wouldn't take any advice from Evelyn. As for Keith's ex, what would make you think he's not over her?"

I bit into a honey-glazed chicken wing and shrugged. "I'm not sure. I just know that he really cared a lot about her."

"So, in other words, you're fishing. Trying to find anything that you can to justify why you're acting this way toward him. All I can say, Trina, is that if you love him, and I know you do, don't let him get away. In my heart, I seriously feel as if he is the one for you. There is something about him that is intriguing to me. Don't blow it by listening to Evelyn. Her advice isn't worth two cents."

I kept trying to talk myself out of calling Keith or going to see him, but Kayla insisted that I do something fast. I took her advice, and after we ended our long conversation over dinner, she went her way and I went mine. We made plans to get together again, over the weekend.

Since Keith's house was only fifteen minutes away, I drove to it. I started to call and let him know that I was coming over, but I decided against it. Instead, I made my way to the front door and rang the doorbell. Several lights were on inside, and I heard a bunch of laughter. I then saw Keith step out from the living room with a happy-go-lucky smile on his face. When he saw me, his face fell flat. He opened the door, and that was when I could hear several people talking and music playing.

"I guess I came at a bad time," I said. "Maybe I should've called."

"It would have been nice, but since you're here, feel free to come in."

Since he'd said it like that, I started not to. But just to be nosy, I stepped inside and followed him into the living room. To my surprise, Bryson was there, two other friends of Keith, Jerry and Lance, and Evelyn. She sat close to Bryson with a drink in her hand. It looked as if they were playing cards, and according to Lance, they had a good game going.

"Why don't you join us?" Lance said to me. "Your man needs all the help he can get."

"Tell me about it," Evelyn said, laughing. "And hello, my dear friend. Had I known you were coming over, we could have ridden together."

Seriously? I couldn't believe this trick. Now, I had spoken to Evelyn several times this week and earlier today. Not once did she mention that she was coming over here, or that she and

Bryson had hooked up. It was apparent that they had; otherwise, she wouldn't have been damn near sitting on his lap. It also pissed me off that Keith hadn't said anything to me about her coming over here either. I knew they didn't expect me to just grab a seat and pretend that everything was cool. I wasn't sure who was going to catch hell first. Then again, yes, I was.

"Evelyn, can I speak to you for a minute in the kitchen?"

She uncrossed her legs and rubbed her finger along the side of Bryson's face. "I'll be right back," she said. "Don't let them win, please. If you do, I'm going to cancel those plans we talked about earlier."

The men laughed and all eyes were on Evelyn as she paraded away in her mini-dress, which barely covered her ass. All eyes except for Keith's, who looked in another direction—only because I was there. I stormed into the kitchen with Evelyn in tow. As soon as we entered, I swung around and let her have it.

"Just what in the hell do you think you're doing?" I asked.

As expected, she played clueless. "Wha . . . what do you mean? I'm playing cards. That's what I'm doing."

"Playing cards inside of my man's house without telling me that you were coming over here? How many times have you been here without me knowing it?"

Evelyn rolled her eyes and caught an attitude with me. "Several times, but does it matter? I don't have to tell you everywhere I go. Like, where do they do that at? Stop being so freaking jealous and calm the hell down."

"Jealous? Uh, no. And hell yes, it matters, because I don't appreciate you being here while I'm not. This is real tacky on your part, Evelyn, and it makes no sense for you to keep running over here, even if it is to meet up with Bryson. He has a place and so do you."

"Yeah, we do, but Keith has the best place of all. You know that for yourself. That's why you're always over here. But I guess you're going to knock his brother for wanting to be over here too. How ridiculous is that?"

"Not ridiculous at all, especially when I smell a motive."

"Yeah, well, I smell something too, but it's not coming from me. It's a bunch of bullshit, coming from you. As a reminder, you were the one who called it quits with Keith. I happen to be trying to make a connection with Bryson, and he is the one who decided to come over here. I'm sorry if my little visit has rubbed you the wrong way, but for the last time, get a grip, please."

I wanted to punch Evelyn in her mouth, so she'd never be able to speak again. We continued to go at it, and as we got louder, Keith came into the kitchen.

"What's going on in here?" he asked with a twisted face.

Evelyn threw her hands up in the air. "Honestly, I do not know. Your ex-girlfriend is acting like she going through menopause. Otherwise, I can't explain this bizarre behavior of hers."

"You know damn well what my problem is, so don't stand there and play innocent. Like I said, I don't appreciate you being over here, and the fact that you don't even have any panties on concerns me."

Evelyn's mouth grew wide. "Whether I have on panties or not, that shouldn't concern you at all. You act like you want a piece of my pussy for yourself, but unfortunately, I have it reserved for Bryson. Now, if you don't mind, I'd like to get back to the card game. That's unless Keith prefers that I leave, and he hasn't said anything of that nature to me yet."

Evelyn looked at Keith and so did I. But before I gave him a chance to respond, I had to reply to Evelyn's comment. "Tramp, I wouldn't dare tamper with a pussy as used up as yours. Bryson can have it. I'm sure it won't be long before he throws it back into the water and searches for something more refreshing." I turned to Keith. "With that being said, we need some privacy tonight. Do you mind asking everyone to leave?"

Unfortunately, Keith wasn't having it. He moved his head from side to side. "If you want privacy, we can go upstairs. I'm not asking my guests to leave, and I would like for you to take your tone down a notch and stop all this cussing."

A smirk washed across Evelyn's face. She turned around and marched her prissy ass out of the kitchen. My feelings were bruised, and my anger was now directed toward Keith.

"I am shocked. I seriously thought you cared about me. Obviously not."

"Trina, stop being so difficult. If you have something on your mind, let's go upstairs and discuss whatever it is. I'm not going to stand here and discuss my business in front of everyone. Nor am I going to ask my brother and my friends to leave because you decided to show up without calling. For some reason, your insecurities are taking over, and you have no reason, whatsoever, to feel insecure around me."

I lifted my finger and pointed it near his face. "This has nothing to do with me being insecure.

I have my reasons for not wanting my friends in your house, but . . . never mind." I moved around Keith and headed toward the kitchen's doorway. He reached for my arm to stop me.

"Calm down, all right? You have got to stop all of this madness. Please tell me what has got you so on edge like this."

I didn't respond, so Keith took my hand. He led the way, and as we walked past the living room, I saw Evelyn sitting close to Bryson again. She sipped from the glass of wine and laughed as if she was having the best time ever.

"You are a cheater," Bryson said to her. "I don't play with women who cheat."

That hookah was way more than that. If he only knew how she really was.

Keith and I went all the way up the stairs to his studio. I guess he didn't want anyone to hear me yelling or cussing him out. I hadn't intended on going there, until I sat on the couch and saw a sketch that was on his workstation. He tried to snatch it up, but his hands weren't quicker than my eyes.

"Please tell me that I didn't just see what I think I saw."

"What did you see?"

Why in the hell did he opt to go there? See, these were the kinds of games that I didn't have time for. He knew damn well what I was talking about. To stand there and try to play clueless infuriated me even more. I tried to snatch the sketchpad from his hand, but he held it up high so I wouldn't get it.

"Listen," he said as I stood in front of him. "I forgot all about this. The last thing I need is for you to get the wrong idea. This sketch is totally innocent, and I drew it spur of the moment."

I held out my hand. "Let me see it."

Keith sighed and gave the sketch to me. As I suspected, it was a sketch of Evelyn. I swallowed the lump in my throat and tossed the sketch on the couch.

"Do you care to tell me when you did that? Or did it happen during one of her several visits over here?"

Keith had a look on his face as if this was going to be difficult for him to explain. He massaged his hands together, shifted his eyes to the doorway, sighed, and then responded, "She stopped by to get Bryson's phone number. That's when I did the sketch."

"How does a person who stops by to get a phone number, wind up sitting on the couch in your studio with her legs crossed, and getting sketched?"

"I invited her to come upstairs to see my artwork."

"What else did you invite her to see? I mean, why not your bedroom?"

"Trina, stop it. It wasn't even like that."

"How do I know it wasn't? All of a sudden, she's showing up at your house, being all chummy and shit with you and your friends. Then I find out that she's been on the same couch that you done screwed me on time and time again. Not to mention that her phone number is on the sketch, too, Keith. This ain't looking too good, and I honestly don't trust you or her."

"If you truly believe that I've been having sex with your friend, then there is no reason for this conversation to continue. It's bad enough that you don't even trust me anymore, but to suggest that I'm fucking your friend is pretty low."

"Before you say anything else, all I ask is that you flip the script. Put yourself in my shoes. You walk into your friend's house and see a sketched picture of me on his table. Not once has he mentioned that I visited him before, but he took it upon himself to sketch a picture of me. How would you feel?"

"Honestly?"

"I wouldn't accept your response any other way."

"Honestly, I wouldn't be mad. If he's considered my friend, I would trust him. Just like I

would trust that you wouldn't go there with him.
I would think that he drew the picture for me, or
something like that."

I was blunt. "Bullshit, Keith, and you know it.
The question is, why did you sketch the picture
anyway? I truly don't get it."

To me, he looked to be fishing for an answer.
Whatever his explanation was, I wasn't buying
it. "I sketched it for Bryson. I was going to play a
joke on him by sending him the picture, since he
said he couldn't resist her."

My eye twitched as I stared at Keith. "Apparently, you couldn't resist her. That was a bunch
of crap you just said, but it doesn't even matter
anymore. I'm out of here. I truly regret coming
here to mend things with you."

I walked out, and as I had expected, Keith
didn't come after me. I was pissed, too, and I
couldn't wait to call Kayla to tell her just how
wrong her advice was.

Chapter 9

Evelyn

Bryson and I had been seeing a lot of each other. Keith had given him my number, and I received a phone call later that day. We met up and clicked instantly, had a wonderful dinner at Outback Steakhouse; and then we went downtown to walk around. We talked about everything from his fiancée, who he wasn't really feeling, to his career that he loved very much. He and Keith were very close, and their parents, as well as their grandparents who had died and left Keith that house, were wealthy people.

Needless to say, I felt like I'd hit the jackpot. I explained my unfortunate financial situation to Bryson, and I told him how difficult it had been for me to find a job. Almost immediately thereafter, he got on the phone and made some phone calls. He set up an interview for me at the construction company he worked for. An administrative assistant position was open, and it paid $40,000 a year. That wasn't enough money to get overly hyped about, but I couldn't turn down the job right now. Plus, I had an opportunity to work close with Bryson. As the construction manager, he spent some of his time in the office, too. I was pleased about that. It would allow me the opportunity to keep my eyes on him.

Later that day, I drove to Bryson's condo for a quick dinner. I wanted to thank him for helping to get me a job, and he also loaned me $1,000 to assist with my rent. My landlord was happy to receive it. I told him I'd be starting a new job, so he backed off, knowing that I might be able to pay my rent on time.

Bryson popped a bottle of champagne and plopped down on the couch. He put the bottle up to his lips and guzzled down the champagne like it was water. When he finished, he slammed the bottle on the table and belched.

"Ahhh, you didn't want any of that, did you?" he said in a playful manner.

I moved closer to him on the sectional couch and threw my leg over his. I wiggled his tie loose and pulled it away from his neck.

"Champagne doesn't excite me as much as you do. And I prefer to have, or should I say give you a little something to show you how appreciative I am for the job and for the money you loaned me. I promise to pay it back, and I can't thank you enough."

Bryson smiled as I removed his tie and started to unbutton his crisp white shirt. We hadn't had sex yet, but there was surely a lot of sexting going on between us. I was eager to find out what he was working with.

"Evelyn, I have a feeling that you're going to get me in a whole lot of trouble. You're so damn sexy, and I'm looking forward to you serving me, every chance you get."

As I moved Bryson's shirt away from his chest and got a glimpse of his bulging muscles and tight abs, the pleasure would be all mine. There were no tattoos on his chest, like Keith's, and I had to admit that Bryson was a tad bit sexier. I maneuvered myself between his legs and got on my knees. While looking into his light brown eyes that were slightly slanted, I unlatched his leather belt. I pulled it away from his cut waistline and eased his zipper over the growing hump in his black slacks. Within seconds, his dick grew tall and escaped through the slit in his boxers. I touched the tip of it with my long fingernails then gripped it tight.

"Nice," I said. "And thick and juicy, just how I like it."

Bryson snickered and kept his eyes glued to me, awaiting my next move. That consisted of my mouth opening wide and covering his entire muscle. I saw his head drop back, and it wasn't long before his eyes closed. His hand touched the back of my head, and as I sucked him in to the back of my throat, he patted my neck and squeezed it.

"Mmmmm," he moaned and lifted himself just a little to stroke my mouth. It was moving pretty fast, along with my hands. My saliva covered every inch of him, and he was so far down my throat that I thought I'd choke. But sucking dick was my specialty. I knew how to make a man's eyes roll to the back of his head. I perfected how to make his toes curl, and it wouldn't take long for his semen to shoot up like fireworks. Bryson was no exception. Within two minutes, I felt his grip on my neck tighten. He also yanked my hair, and his thrusts into my mouth were now at a speedy pace.

"Suck that shit, baby. Swallow all of it and don't let one fucking drop go to waste."

My mouth swelled like a balloon as he released his juices inside of it. I didn't swallow all of it, but I licked some of the drippings from his pretty dick, which was now limp.

"Ahhhhh," Bryson moaned again. His six pack fluttered and sweat beads rested on his stomach. I licked around the minimal, smooth hair above his dick, and then sucked my fingers.

"Now that," I said, "was tasty."

Bryson sat up and leaned forward. He brought his lips to my glossy ones and our tongues danced for a while. During the intense kiss, he reached for my hand and placed it on his muscle. I felt it swelling, but it wasn't as hard as it was the first time.

"Stroke it," he said, backing away from my lips. "It'll get there."

"I'm sure it will, but I have a better idea."

I stood and unbuttoned the royal blue silk blouse that I wore. Within seconds, the blouse, my bra, and my tight skirt were in a pile next to me. All I stood in was a turquoise thong and my moisturized caramel skin glistened. Bryson's eyes scanned my plump breasts, which were sitting pretty. Then his eyes lowered to the tiny gap between my lips. My shaved slit was clearly visible, and it was inviting as well.

"You gon' make me hurt you, woman," he said. "Perfection. Pure perfection."

I couldn't have agreed with him more. He got up and laid me back on the couch. While bending over me, he reached for my panties and pulled them over my high-heeled shoes. He removed those as well, and tossed them over his shoulders. We both laughed, and before he did away with his slacks, he reached for a condom.

"You don't mind, do you?" he said, already putting it on. "I definitely don't want any children, and it's always good to be safe."

I agreed, but I damn sure wouldn't mind having his child. His wealthy parents would spoil the baby. I was sure I would somehow benefit too. Not to mention all that Bryson would probably do. But regardless, we went at it. He wrapped my legs around his back and positioned his dick at the crevasses of my hole. It wasn't long before he snaked his thickness inside of me, causing my pussy lips to spread wide. Probably wider than they had ever been before, because I could definitely feel his meat stretching my insides. I released one of my legs from his waist and poured it over his shoulder. I had to represent how flexible I was, so I pointed my leg out straight, as if I were doing a split. Bryson tackled my goodies down below, and with each perfectly planned thrust, my pussy juices ran over. His shaft was glazed from top to bottom. We both watched his insertions, and I was so hot and bothered that I began to massage my own clit. Bryson licked his lips to prevent saliva from dripping from his mouth. His eyes fluttered, his breathing increased and his soft moans let me know just how good my pussy felt to him. I reached around to grip his solid ass, and all I felt was sweat. At the pace we were going, things were starting to get heated. Our naked, wet bodies slapped together, and as he sucked the shit out of my breasts, a high arch formed in my back.

"Brrrryson," I cried out near tears. "I . . . My pussy would like to thank you for all of this. It feels guuuud, damn, you're making us feel sooooo guuud."

Bryson didn't have a comeback, but his actions let me know that he felt the same way. He eased out of me, and as a flood of my juices ran onto the couch, all he could do was shake his head. He sat up straight and positioned me to stand in front of him with my back to him. I did so with straddled legs. Cum trickled down between my thighs, while Bryson massaged them. He also massaged my ass then he held my waist and motioned for me to squat. His dick stood straight up, ready to aim and shoot.

"Ease down on it," he said. "And I won't complain if you drive me into overtime."

He must've known how I operated. I definitely drove us into overtime by riding him backward. I then got on my hands and knees on the floor, and allowed Bryson to have anal sex with me. An hour and a half in, we were spent. We passed out on the carpeted floor, and I wasn't sure who had more carpet burns, him or me.

I was still knocked out. Bryson was too, until we heard hard knocks on his door. My leg was thrown over his and the smell of sex infused the air. I was so sticky between my legs. A shower was definitely what I needed, but it didn't appear that I was going to get it anytime soon.

"Damn," Bryson said, getting off the floor. We both looked at the clock; it showed two thirty-five in the morning. The hard knocks continued, so Bryson turned to me.

"Do you mind going into my bedroom?" he asked. "I have a feeling that I know who this is."

"No problem." I got off the floor and moved into his bedroom. The king bed was neatly made and the soft comforter felt soothing against my naked body. I started to go by the door to listen in, but I could already hear the voice of a woman speaking.

"All day, Bryson," she said. "I've been trying to reach you all day."

"I had every intention of calling you back, but I got tied up. And I told you before about showing up like this. We agreed to go our separate ways for a while, and with you showing up like this, it doesn't help."

"It doesn't help you, because you're always up to no good. We will never be able to fix our relationship if you refuse to answer your phone so we can talk about it. And while we agreed to go our separate ways for a while, that didn't mean we were supposed to stop communicating, did it?"

I rolled my eyes at this stupid heifer. I mean, how many women had to beg and plead with a man to get his shit right? Bryson's ass didn't need space. What he needed was more excitement in his life and some more pussy. I had a thing for men like him, but, at least, I knew from the beginning what I was dealing with. And while the dick was always beneficial to me, it had to come attached with money. Good dick without money wasn't worth my time.

As expected, the tears came into play. I could hear the woman crying about how Bryson had been so mean and disrespectful to her.

"You haven't done anything for me. You played me. I saw you with her . . ."

The ranting went on and on about why he didn't do this or that, and he didn't seem to care anymore. If so, then why in the hell was she standing in his condo at almost three o'clock in the morning, eager to repair their relationship? I just didn't get it, and I despised women who were too stupid to realize that most men didn't give a damn about those tears.

"What else can I do?" she cried. "You say that you love me, and that we're going to get married. But when, Bryson? Please tell me when."

"N-e-v-e-r," I said in a whisper. According to Bryson, they'd been engaged for four years. If it hadn't happened by now, didn't she know she was wasting her time? I wanted to scream at the top of my lungs, but I didn't have to. I heard some tussling going on, and a few seconds later, the woman came busting into the room. I was surprised to see that she was white.

Her teary eyes fluttered as she saw me sitting on the bed with no clothes on. She looked as if she wanted to pass out. She covered her mouth, as if this was really a surprise to her. By how calm Bryson was, I could tell this wasn't the first time he'd been busted. He held her shoulders, massaging them, as she sobbed and appeared to weaken.

"Libby, go home," he said in a smooth, calm tone. "We'll talk about this tomorrow, okay? Don't do this to yourself *again*."

Libby choked up even more. The look in my eyes dared her to say anything smart to me. If she did, she would catch hell. She doubled over and held her stomach.

"Why?" she cried out. "Why do you keep doing this to meeeee?"

Was she asking me why? If so, her answer was simple. Because her dumb ass let him. I had no sympathy for her, but apparently, Bryson did. He eased his arms around her waist to hold her up. He continued to smooth talk his way out of this.

"Come on, Libby. Calm down, baby, and get yourself together. You don't have to do this. You know who I love. All I wanted to do was have a little fun, since we were separated. You know it wouldn't go down like this, if we were together."

"But you can have all the fun you want to with meeeee. Why her, Bryson, why her?"

What did she mean by why her? Did she have to ask? I mean, look at me. All she had to do was look at how gorgeous I was. Damn.

Bryson continued to hold her by the waist. He escorted her into the bathroom so she could get herself together. On their way there, he looked over Libby's shoulder and shrugged. Behind the concerned expression on his face was also a smirk.

Some men got a kick out of this shit; it made them feel special. There was no question in my mind that Bryson was one of those men. It would be a cold day in hell if he ever got me to react this way.

While in the bathroom, he washed Libby's face and patted it with a towel. He insisted that she stay calm, and then he asked her, again, to go home.

"I'll call you first thing in the morning. We'll have breakfast, and how about I make you some of those favorite blueberry pancakes you like?"

She sniffled and slowly nodded. I swear I wanted to get off the bed and go knock some sense into her. I don't believe that God intended for some women to be this damn stupid. This chick was worse than Kayla, and I didn't believe it got any worse than her. Black dick had the minds of many all fucked up.

Bryson held on tight to Libby as he escorted her toward the door. She gave me a quick roll of her eyes, but didn't say one word to me. I comfortably sat back on the bed with my hands behind me, my breasts poked out and my legs crossed. Minutes later, I heard the front door shut, and Bryson rushed back into the bedroom.

"I am so sorry about that. That shit caught me off guard. I thought that she and I had an understanding."

"No problem. Handle your business, baby. As long as it doesn't interfere with what we have going on, I'm good."

He crawled on the bed and held himself up over me. "I'll tell you who has got it going on. You do. The way you're looking on my bed, all sexy and shit like this, makes me want to eat you alive."

"You may not be able to do that, especially since you have to get up in a few hours to make those blueberry pancakes. I don't like to be rushed, and I assume that I'll be asked to leave soon."

"Nope. As a matter of fact, I can make you some of those pancakes too. They're delicious, and for some reason, Libby can't seem to get enough of them."

Arrogant motherfucker, I thought. He was nothing like Keith was, but I had to settle. "Scrap the pancakes," I said. "Not interested. But I am interesting in seeing how well you can eat me alive."

"I can show you better than I can tell you."

Bryson parted my legs and buried his face between them. His eating skills were decent, but he damn sure was no Cedric. I closed my eyes and pretended, just for a few minutes, that he was. Then I went into a daze, thinking about how much fun Cedric and I used to have during sex. More so, how creative we were, even while Kayla was in the same vicinity as we were.

That day, we were all at Kayla's and Cedric's house having dinner. I'd brought a date, trying to make Cedric jealous. He turned out to be a disaster, and as we were all downstairs playing pool and watching reality TV shows, I made my way up the stairs to find Cedric. The moment I reached the top stair, Cedric was standing by the kitchen counter waiting for me. He placed one finger over his lips, as a gesture for me to be quiet. He then nudged his head toward the garage door and walked toward it. I followed, laughing my ass off about what we were about to do. Inside of the five-car garage was a fleet of lavish cars that belonged to him and Kayla. The only spot that was empty was the spot where Jacoby parked his car. Cedric unlocked the car, and he opened the back door to his Rolls-Royce that provided plenty of room in the back seat.

"Are you serious?" I whispered to him. "We're just going to talk, aren't we?"

"Ay, that's all I want to do, unless you have something else in mind like hooking me up."

We chuckled, and I got in the back seat with Cedric. Talking wasn't in our plans. His hands eased up my thigh-high skirt, and the moment his fingers slipped into my wetness, I turned on my stomach. Cedric unzipped his pants and flipped up the back of my skirt. He moved my thong to the side and filled my hot pocket with his hard, thick meat that always guaranteed me an orgasm.

"You know I'm jealous," Cedric whispered in my ear while long stroking me from behind. My ass was hiked up. The sounds of my pussy juices made him aware that he was hitting the right spot.

"Jealous of who or whaaaat?" I moaned. "You have noooo reason to be jealous. I'm the one who is jealous. Jealous of Kayla for getting a piece of this whenever she wants to."

"You can have a piece whenever you want to too. Just ask for it. And the next time you come over here, leave the broke-looking joker at home. He should be an embarrassment to you. I know you can do much better."

"I can. That's why I'm doing it with you and not with him."

Cedric tore into my insides and rushed me to the finish line so we could hurry to go back inside. The car rocked fast from the speed of our action, but as soon as I opened my mouth to react to him busting my cherry, the garage door lifted. Cedric covered my mouth with his hand and we dropped low on the floor in the back seat. My pussy was dripping wet from a mixture of our juices, and the feel of Cedric's dick still in me felt spectacular.

More than anything, I wished that Kayla would have come into the garage and seen us. Cedric peeked through the tinted windows and whispered to me that it was Jacoby, not Kayla. He waited until Jacoby was inside before he hit me with a few more strokes that tickled my insides and gave me something more to smile about. He had definitely gotten what he wanted. Now, it was time for me to get what I wanted. That, of course, was his money. Money that I could never get off my mind, because it was the way to my prosperity.

Cedric agreed to give me some money that day, and after our creative little sex session, we entered the house as if nothing had gone on between us. I sat right next to Kayla with Cedric's scent all over me. She had to know what the deal was, didn't she? Well, if she didn't know, I certainly did.

I also knew that I'd have to go see about Cedric real soon, because men like Bryson just wasn't going to cut it. If I was going to involve myself with a real player, why not shoot for the best, or should I say, shoot for the player with the most money and the best sex? Compared to Cedric, Bryson was an amateur. I intended to toy with him for a little while longer, but his time would be up sooner than I originally thought.

Chapter 10

Kayla

After days and days of pondering, hours of lost sleep, going back and forth about my marriage, I'd finally made my decision. I was excited about it, too, and the first person that I needed to speak to was Cedric. We had a lot to discuss, so therefore, I made my way to his place.

Jacoby was at school. He and I had a long talk about how much he'd been skipping and his late nights with Adrianne. He admitted everything to me, and his excuse was him being affected, a little, by all that had been going on. He said that Adrianne had truly been there for him, and that he felt so much love when she was around. As for school, he said his work had suffered because he couldn't think straight. I understood everything he'd said, but I told him it was time for him to get back on track.

The same applied to me and Cedric. That was why I was at his front door. It was time to do this. I made sure Cynthia was out of the house, and when I entered, I went upstairs to find Cedric.

He wasn't in bed where he normally was, and when I checked the kitchen, family room, and his office, he wasn't there either. That was when I went to the lower level and saw him in the workout room, slowly jogging on the treadmill. He appeared to be getting himself back in shape, and I had to admit that he looked dynamite in his tan shorts. He didn't have on a shirt, and plenty of muscles bulged from his shoulders and toned calves. His beard was still a little scruffy, but his fade was intact. Every time I watched Scandal and would see Columbus Short, he always reminded me of my husband. Loud music played and Cedric looked up at the flat-screen TV mounted on the wall, as if he could hear it. I walked in and turned the music down.

"Good morning," I said then sat on a weight bench. "I see you must be feeling better."

"Much better."

He slowed down the treadmill then got off of it. He used a fluffy towel to wipe his face then stood in front of me. Sweat dripped from his body and the shorts hung low on his waist.

I could see the bullet wound on his chest, and all I could think about was how lucky he was to be alive. I reached out to touch the wound. "Does it hurt?" I asked.

"It's still a little tender right there, but not really. I've been taking good care of myself since then. Been eating right, exercising, and playing with my dick to keep it alive and active too." Cedric winked and laughed.

I rolled my eyes and shook my head. "That's too much information, but I'm glad you're feeling better. Looking much better, too."

He nodded and looked me up and down. I had on a simple pair of tight jeans and a button-down shirt that matched my yellow earrings. My hair had been trimmed, nails had been done, and my sandals showed my perfect pedicure.

"So do you," Cedric complimented. "And just so you know, I do love your hair like that."

"Thanks." I moved away from him and rubbed my hands together. I was a little nervous, but I assumed that he knew what I was there to discuss.

"Would you like to go upstairs to my office?" he suggested. "That way, you can sit on the couch and relax."

I nodded. "Yes. That sounds perfect."

I made my way up the stairs with Cedric following me.

"At least I know *that's* still in working order," he said.

When we reached the top stair, I turned with confusion on my face. "What did you say? I'm not sure wha—"

"I was talking about my manhood. It had a reaction when you were walking in front of me."

I moved out of the way and gestured for Cedric to go in front of me. "That's good to know. Maybe I'll have some kind of reaction too, walking behind you."

We laughed and made our way to his office. I sat on the couch, while Cedric stood with his backside against the desk and his arms folded.

"So, what's the verdict? Don't give me a long spiel either. All I need for you to do is hit me with your news and so be it."

"I don't know if I can sum this up as quickly as you may want me to, but the first thing I think you should know is that Evelyn had an abortion. She thought that you were dead, and since she couldn't provide for the baby, she terminated the pregnancy. I wasn't sure if you knew that."

Cedric didn't flinch. "No, I didn't know, but thanks for sharing. I'll toast later, but for now, I want to discuss you and me. What's the deal?"

"Cutting to the chase, the deal is, I want to proceed with the divorce."

This time, Cedric flinched. He cocked his neck from side to side, and I saw him take a hard swallow.

"That's your final decision?"

"Yes, it is. I just don't see how we can ever get this to work out, and I do believe that this is one of those cases where there has been too much damage done."

"I agree, but whatever happened to for better or worse? We had our worse, Kayla, and we had to kind of go through some things in order to get to this point. Now, don't get me wrong. I respect your decision, but I'm trying to get you to see that many things, a lot of things, have changed."

"I think they have, Cedric, but I don't believe that those changes will be enough for me. So, I'll just take my measly, little, tiny twenty percent and go on my merry way."

Cedric chuckled and rubbed his brow. "I figured you'd go there with that twenty percent. But, remember, if you stay, you can have waaay more than that."

"If I stay, that may be true. But then I'd have to deal with your late hours again, concern myself with who you're with, check your bank accounts, go through your pockets, hire private detectives, just to make sure you're staying on the up-and-up. I don't want to live my life like that anymore. It's time for me to be happy and live peacefully. I deserve that."

"You absolutely do, so I can't argue with you on that."

Cedric walked around his desk and sat in the chair. He typed on his keyboard, and seconds later, his printer sounded off. He removed the piece of paper and laid it flat on his desk. Whatever it was he signed it, and then brought the paper over to me. It was the last page of the dissolution of marriage agreement I had read time and time again.

"The signature you provided before wasn't acceptable because you were under the influence of alcohol. If you say what you mean, your signature is needed."

I took the paper from his hand and held it. "First of all, I'ma need you to change that twenty percent to at least forty percent, print off the whole agreement, and give me a signed copy, and then get a notary in here to notarize it, until our attorneys can confirm."

Cedric cracked up and walked back over to his desk. "I can't get you a notary right now, and there will be no problem with our attorneys confirming this. Also, I will be happy to give you a signed copy, but unfortunately, the twenty percent stands because you're the one abandoning me."

I stood and went over to his desk. "For a very good reason, I may add, so let's crank that amount up to, at least, thirty-eight percent for my troubles."

"Twenty-two."

"Thirty-six."

"Twenty-five."

"Thirty-three."

"Thirty and that's my final offer."

I sighed and released a tiny smile. "Thirty will do, and anything is better than twenty."

"Sixty-nine then. Over there, on the couch with you on top."

"No, thanks. And why are you being so nasty today? We're supposed to be down in the dumps today, sad and disappointed that we're ending this. You seem just as happy as I am."

Cedric looked at me with a blank expression. "Happy, I'm not, but I'm trying to make the best of this situation. I hope you are too."

"More than you know."

Cedric printed two copies of the document and we both signed it. "There you go, Miss Lady," he said. "After one lump-sum payment, I can finally be rid of you and have you out of my hair."

"I doubt that because we still have a son to raise. You know he's been getting away with murder in my absence, and I think we're going to have to put our feet down."

"I've seen his sneaky self in action. But let him go ahead and do what teenagers do. Eventually, he'll learn some valuable lessons that will either lift him up, or bring him down."

"Yeah, that's what I'm afraid of. Now come here."

Cedric stood next to me and I put my face next to his. I held up the agreement and told him to smile while I used my cell phone to take a selfie of us.

"You're crazy," he said with a fake frown. I was all smiles when I snapped the picture.

"I may need to send this picture to someone. Thanks."

Cedric moved away from me, but we stayed in his office, talking for about another hour. He agreed to wire the lump-sum payment into my account by tomorrow, but said that he needed to go directly to the bank in order to transfer that kind of money. We also talked about living arrangements. His intentions were to put the house up for sale and move into a smaller place. I was planning to get me a place as well. Jacoby was left to decide who he wanted to live with, and Cedric and I were fine with that. The truth was, I hadn't felt this good in a long time. I was glad that we'd gotten closure. Now I could focus on my own life. Holding on for so long had only crippled me.

I made my way to the front door so I could leave. Cedric was behind me. "I guess I'll see you whenever," he said.

I turned and gave him a tight hug. He rubbed my back and I rubbed his. I felt his hardness, but backed away from him.

"Now, who would've thought that my ex-wife was capable of doing this to me?" He looked down at his rising shorts. "All I can say is, baby, you're bad in every way possible. Why don't we seal the deal by indulging in some of that wild sex we used to have when we were mad at each other? You were always at your best when you were mad at me, and I would be thinking about that shit for days and weeks after."

I couldn't help but to laugh at Cedric's attempt to have sex with me. "Sex or no sex, the deal is sealed. And I'm not really mad at you now, so having sex would be a waste of time. So, good-bye, Cedric. I'm sure we'll be speaking soon. Please don't forget about the money tomorrow because I really need it. If you need me to take you to the bank, let me know."

I reached for the doorknob and Cedric smacked me on my ass; squeezed it too, and had the nerve to honk. I made my exit and closed the door behind me. But when I got into the car, I sat for a while thinking. I looked at the bay windows, manicured lawn, and two-story brick house that was one of the best looking houses on the block. Cedric had taken good care of me, no doubt. It was kind of painful to leave here for good, knowing that I would never officially stay in the house again. With that in mind, I wanted to leave my mark. I marched toward the front door and opened it. Went inside and made my way up the stairs where I could hear water running. Right at the bedroom's doorway, I removed all of my clothes and then swished toward the bathroom where Cedric stood naked, waiting for the tub to fill. His eyes shifted to me in the doorway, and a wide smile washed across his face.

"I guess this ain't really over, until it's over," he said.

"Oh, it's over, trust me. I just had an urge to seal the deal, like you suggested."

I walked into the bathroom and threw my arms around Cedric's shoulders. With our bodies pressed together, both of our hands roamed. Cedric touched my curvy backside, and I had my hand on his heavy, hard meat. Just as I was about to direct it inside of me, he stopped me.

"You'd better not tell your girlfriends about this. If so, they would think you're out of your mind."

"What I do with my life is my business. I don't owe anybody an explanation; after all, no one has walked in my shoes. If I want to screw my ex-husband's brains out, I will."

"Then g'on with your bad self. And you're right. To hell with them all. We got this."

I wasn't sure about the "we" thing, but I surely did have it. Got all of it and then some. And right after we finished having sex, I thanked Cedric for the good loving and made my exit with my divorce papers in hand.

This time when I got in the car, I drove off. I reached for my cell phone to call Trina and share the good news. She didn't seem as upbeat as she did the last time.

"Okay, what's going on?" I asked, feeling a little frustrated. Just once, one time, I wanted to talk to somebody who didn't have a lot of drama going on.

"If I told you, you wouldn't believe me. All I can say is I shouldn't have ever stopped by Keith's house that night. Then again, I'm glad I did because I discovered that your friend has been making her rounds."

My brows arched inward. "What friend? I don't have many, so who are you talking about?"

"Evelyn. Do you know she was at Keith's house when I got there?"

I had to slam on the brakes. "Are you kidding me?"

"No, I'm not. She's supposed to be seeing Keith's brother, but I found a picture that Keith sketched of her while she was sitting on the couch in his studio. He pretended that it wasn't a big deal, but Evelyn made it clear that she had been there, several times, when I wasn't. Keith thinks I'm overreacting, but you already know how Evelyn is."

"Yes, I do. And I'm surprised at Keith. I don't know what to say about Evelyn, but the two of us need to do something to put that chick in her place. I don't understand why you continue to be her friend. I am soooo done with her. That hooker can't say anything to me right about now."

"I question why I keep fooling with her too, but this last incident took the cake. She called and tried to apologize for upsetting me, but she wouldn't admit to doing the wrong thing. Said there was no harm in her going over there. When I inquired about the sketch, she said she didn't know Keith was doing it, until he was finished. She also said that he made some advances toward her. I'm so upset right now that I don't even want to bring any of this shit to his attention."

"I think you should. At least give him a chance to explain himself. Evelyn lies so much, Trina. You can't believe everything she says."

"I agree, but it's his reaction that has me more bothered than anything. He hasn't called, he hasn't apologized, nothing. I'm not going to reach out to him again, so it's whatever. Now, enough about my drama. What's going on with you? Did you make a decision yet?"

I shared with Trina everything that had gone down with me and Cedric, including the sex. She barked through the phone and laughed at my actions.

"You are so trifling, but good for you. You're sounding much better, and I think this calls for a celebration. Let's go somewhere this weekend and get our party on. Have a few drinks and just let it all hang out! We need some more fun in our lives."

"I couldn't agree with you more. Sounds like a plan to me! You name the place and I will be there!"

Trina said she would call me on Friday to let me know our destination. I was excited about hanging with my BFF, and I couldn't wait until the weekend. And before I forgot, I looked at the selfie I'd taken with Cedric. I typed in a number and sent it right over to Evelyn so she could see it. I was sure she would be just as happy as I was about the divorce.

Chapter 11

Trina

I hadn't been clubbing in a long time. The last time I got all dolled up like this was probably at a funeral. I wasn't sure what to wear, but I opted for a pair of stretch jean leggings, a navy cropped jacket, and a white tank. I could barely walk in the high-heeled pumps I had on, but they made my whole fit look sexier. My layered hair was swooped a bit to the left, and I accessorized with red and silver jewelry. I never liked to wear a lot of makeup, so all I did was gloss my lips and spread my lashes with mascara. My brows were already arched, and after several dashes of sweet perfume, I was ready to go.

I told Kayla that I would meet her at a jazz/R&B joint that was on Washington Avenue. Some of the other artists at the studio mentioned the place, but I hadn't ever been there before. To my surprise, it was nice. The crowd was thirty and older, and the loud music spilling through the speakers had many of people there up on their feet. I couldn't really see, but the spinning white lights from up above gave off some light. The club was decorated with purple, black, yellow, and silver. I always appreciated a colorful atmosphere, and the many colorful paintings on the wall impressed me. So did the humungous dance floor, where people from all races were dancing.

Kayla was supposed to be there at nine, but I didn't see her yet. That was until I looked over at a booth and spotted her sitting next to a white man who was all smiles. She saw me and waved her hand. I walked over to the table and the man sitting next to her stood up.

"You must be Kayla's friend, Trina," he said, yelling over the loud music.

"Yes, I am. And you are?"

"Chris. I saw Kayla when she came through the door and was like, wow. She damn near knocked me off my feet."

Kayla was all smiles. I was too, especially since Chris wasn't all that bad looking. Unfortunately, though, I knew my friend all too well. She wanted black dick, and would never settle for anything less.

"Now that Trina is here," Chris said to Kayla, "would you like to dance?"

"Sure." Kayla scooted out of the booth and made her way to the dance floor with Chris.

I eased into the booth and looked around at the drinks on the table. I could tell Kayla and Chris had been getting it in. She must've gotten here earlier than I'd thought. There was also a bottle of wine on the table, sitting in an ice bucket. I took it upon myself to pour some. Minutes later, an older black man with a slanted, mack-daddy hat on eased into the booth with me.

"I bet you a hundred dollars that you're going to turn me down," he said then sucked his teeth. "If so, please give me a Band-Aid, because I just scraped my knee from falling head over heels for you."

How weak was that? I thought. *Really?* But I had to admit, it was funny. "No, I don't have a Band-Aid nor do I have a hundred dollars. But I assure you that I'm like a Rubik's Cube: The more you play with me, the harder I get."

The nice-looking older man slapped his leg and laughed. "I figured you had a good sense of humor. And something told me to come over here and offer to buy you a drink."

I looked at the drinks on the table. "You know what, I'm good. But maybe if you stop by later, we can dance or something. By the way, what's your name again?"

"Chance. If you take a chance on me, you just may get real lucky."

I winked at him. "Okay, I got it. And thanks again for the sideshow. It's been real."

Chance said he would be back later to dance. As soon as he walked away, I looked for Kayla and Chris on the dance floor. Needless to say, it was hilarious. Kayla was a great dancer, but Chris was all over the place. He was doing some mess that James Brown would do. Had his jacket pulled back and was moving his feet so fast that he was about to trip. I cracked up, and you best believe that after one dance, Kayla called it quits. I saw her say something to him, and then she headed back to the table alone.

Dressed in a white, wide-legged jumpsuit, Kayla eased into the booth with me. She was such a classy chick. I couldn't touch her style if I tried.

"What was that all about?" I asked.

"What? What do you mean?"

"I'm talking about the way he was dancing. Girl, he was all over the place."

"Yeah, he was. But he is . . . nice."

"Maybe so, but not nice enough for you to date, right?"

Kayla sipped from the glass in front of her then shrugged. "I might. Not sure yet."

I pursed my lips. "Don't even try to sell that mess to me. You know good and doggone well that a white man could never get it."

Kayla laughed and placed her finger over her lips. "Shhh, don't tell nobody. You already know that I love the brothas."

"Yes, I do."

We sat for a long while, enjoying each other's company, laughing and drinking. I danced, Kayla danced, and then we sang "Happy Birthday" with the people next to us who were there celebrating. I was tipsy as ever, and as the night went on, I was very flirtatious. I had just finished dancing with Chance, before plopping down in the booth and picking up another drink.

Kayla had a glassy film covering her eyes. She looked at me with a straw close to her lips. "I think you'd better slow it down," she whispered. "Somebody here is keeping a very close eye on you."

Regardless of who it was, I sipped from the glass of Patrón and whispered back at Kayla. "Who?"

"I'm not saying. If you look around, maybe you will see him."

I narrowed my eyes and scanned the room. Didn't see anyone I knew, nor did I notice anyone paying attention to me. "I repeat, who?"

"Look over by the bar. At the very end, there
are three men standing together. One is a dark
chocolate, and he is a sight for drunken eyes.
He's rocking jeans, a V-neck shirt that's hug-
ging those muscles and showing those colorful
tattoos. I swear you'd better straighten up and
get to him, before some of these other chicks do.
Trust me when I say they're on it!"

I snapped my head to look over at the bar and
squinted. Sure enough, there was Keith, Bryson,
and one of his other friends. I hurried to duck in
the booth.

"Damn," I said, pounding my leg. "I need to get
out of here. Doooo, do not want him to see me. I
wonder what he's doing here anyway."

Kayla leaned in closer to me. "Don't be mad
at me, but see, you have a best friend who tends
to poke her nose where it doesn't belong sometimes. I kind of reached out to him earlier and
told him that we'd be here. I kind of felt like—"

I pulled my head back and held up one finger.
"Uh, no. We don't go there, Miss Thing, and you
were sooooo wrong for that. I could cuss you out
right now for interfering, but I do not want to
embarrass the hell out of us right now."

"Well, if you're going to do it, hurry up because
we're about to have some visitors."

My eyes shot up, and Keith, Bryson, and their friend were heading our way. He looked so spectacular that my pussy started to get overly excited before I did. I crossed my legs and turned my head, just so I didn't have to look at him.

"Hello, ladies," Bryson said to both of us. "Y'all got a lot of room in this booth. Mind if we squeeze in, especially since there aren't many open seats?"

"Of course," Kayla said, scooting closer to me.

Bryson moved in next to her and their friend sat next to him. Keith sat on my other side, but his back faced me. He sat with his elbows on his knees, watching the crowds of people dancing. I guess his intentions were to ignore me.

"Kayla, right?" Bryson said to her. "You were the one at the hospital, correct?"

"Yes, I was."

"I remember. I told my knucklehead brother over there to hook me up. I was disappointed to hear that you were married."

Kayla blushed. She was happy to reply, "Not anymore."

Bryson licked his lips and moved closer. I quickly spoke up. "Where's Evelyn, Bryson? I spoke to her the other day, and she mentioned that you'd just left her apartment."

He tried to fire back. "I don't keep tabs on Evelyn. The fact that I was at her apartment doesn't mean anything. I'm here right now, in the presence of a beautiful woman who excited me from the very first time that I saw her."

I kept my mouth shut and let Kayla handle Bryson. He was such a dog, and even though Keith had his issues, they were the total opposite.

"Evelyn?" Kayla said, pretending to be surprised. "You've been dating Evelyn?"

"Nah, I wouldn't exactly say that we're dating. Just chilling and conversing from time to time. Stuff like that; nothing real serious."

"Well, any man who enjoys her conversation definitely wouldn't appreciate mine. Personally, I think she's a tramp, and any penis that has ever been inside of her will never get inside of me."

Surprise, surprise. I didn't know my best friend could be so blunt. Bryson's eyes bugged, Keith turned around to look at Kayla, and the other dude halted his conversation with the chick in the booth beside us to turn around.

"Sorry," Kayla said. "Did I say something wrong?"

"Hell no," I said, snatching up the glass of alcohol in front of me. "I wouldn't let a fool who been up in that touch me either. And if I ever find out that we've shared the same man, it will be bad news for him."

"Ladies, let's not talk about Evelyn right now," Bryson said in a smooth tone. He was eager to change the subject, but Kayla wasn't buying it. Her experience with Cedric left her with a lot of knowledge. It was easy for her to see through the bullshit.

As they talked, I was anxious to move away from Keith.

"Excuse me," I said to him so he'd move.

He stood and eased his hands into his pockets. Before I could get out of the booth, a mixed-looking chick stepped up to him. "Would you like to dance?" she politely asked.

"Sure," he replied. "Why not?"

He walked away and so did I. I tried not to keep my eyes on him, but I couldn't help it. I kept seeing him whisper in the chick's ear and they also kept laughing. I also watched Kayla and Bryson. They appeared to be indulged in an interesting conversation. Both of them kept smiling too. I hoped like hell that she didn't go there. That was definitely a bad move, but I trusted that after her experience with Cedric, she wouldn't give Bryson the time of day.

I went to the restroom to use it then staggered my way through the crowd to take a seat at the bar. It was so hot that my jacket was now sticking to my skin. I was very uncomfortable. I removed my jacket and placed it on the back of a chair. I then ordered another drink, but a young man with dreads sat down next to me, offering to pay for it.

"Don't bother," Keith said reaching over him to place his money on the bar. "I got it."

The dude looked Keith up and down then glanced at me. I didn't say anything, so he shrugged and walked away. Keith sat in his seat.

"So, you're not going to say anything to me," he said. "The least you could do is speak."

"I spoke while we were at the table. You didn't hear me because your back was turned."

"If you spoke, I would have heard you and replied. But whatever. How's everything going with you?"

"Great. Can't complain."

"Hmmm, wish I could say the same. I have a lot to complain about, but I guess now isn't the place or time to do it."

"You're right, it's not. And the thing is, I don't care to listen. Buy that bitch you were dancing with that drink. I'm going home."

I grabbed my jacket from the chair and walked toward the door. Before leaving, I saw that Kayla was still talking to Bryson. I figured that when I got in the car, I would send her a text to tell her why I had to leave. Being in Keith's presence didn't sit right with me.

I pushed the doors open and left the club. Several people were standing outside smoking and talking. One dude whistled at me, but I didn't bother to turn my head. I kept it moving, until someone came up from behind and snatched my arm.

"Okay," Keith said, turning me around to face him. "If a fight is what you want, then you're going to get it. If you want for us to stand out here and embarrass our fucking selves, then that's what we'll do. Throw in a few curse words, attack each other, and then go home still mad. Shall I start this or do you want to?"

I waved him off and kept it moving. "Fuck you, Keith. I don't have time."

He rushed up from behind me again. "Well, that's a start. Fuck you too, and why in the hell were you in there allowing those men to buy you drinks, feel all on you on the dance floor, and pass their numbers to you? I see you haven't wasted no time moving on, and you don't have to tell me again how great your life has been since we parted."

I sped up the pace to get to my car. "Sounds like you're mad. Good. And it's about time you started to show some interest."

"So, through your eyes, I show interest by yelling, screaming, cussing, and acting a fool.

You are confused, baby. So damn confused about how a relationship should really operate. Maybe you do need to hook up with one of those men in there. They can probably offer you what I can't: drama."

I tried to upset Keith by agreeing with him. "Maybe so. And I should have hooked up with somebody, because I don't have a man anymore. See, my man is too busy having open condoms in his medicine cabinet, sketching pictures of my friends and inviting them to come over whenever they wish. Personally, I think his dick has been inside of her, but that's just how I feel."

"Get the hell out of here with that mess. You're just saying that to fuck with me. You want to upset me, just so we can continue to create this scene out here and you can then bring more attention to yourself."

I stopped at my car and removed my keys from my purse. "This scene that you're causing is too weak for me, so I'm going home. If you want someone to listen to your lies, call Evelyn. She knows where you stay. I'm sure she'll be happy to stop by and keep you company."

I unlocked the door and opened it. Keith rushed up to me and slammed the door so hard that it rattled the glass. He grabbed my arms and pushed me against the hood of the car.

"You want a bigger scene," he said through gritted teeth and with much anger locked in his eyes. I thought he was going to strike me, but instead he unlatched his belt, unzipped his jeans, and dropped them to his ankles.

"I'll show your ass a bigger scene all right."

Keith snatched me by the front of my jeans and lifted me. Damn near slamming me on the hood, he yanked at my zipper and attempted to unzip my jeans. I tried to force him away from me by pushing his shoulders back. He was too strong.

"You keep on bringing up that bitch Evelyn's name, but I'll show you who the fuck I want! When I tell you, you don't listen, so I need to show yo' ass the motherfucker who really excites me! Stop fighting back and allow me this one opportunity to create a scene your heart desires! I'ma do it right here, and you better not say shit!"

Keith wasn't playing. He was real rough with me, and when all was said and done, my ripped shirt hung off my shoulder, my jeans and shoes were in the dirt, and my backside was on the hood of the car. Keith was in between my legs and neither of us could catch our breaths. I had my fist tightened on the front of his shirt, grabbing it and telling him to let me go.

"Shut the fuck up. Just shut up and listen." He took deep breaths, but his voice was calmer. His forehead dripped with sweat and it was dotted with beads of sweat. "I have been so miserable without you. Sick to my damn stomach, trying to figure out where in the hell did I go wrong. All I asked was for you to move in with me. For whatever reason, that shit set off a firestorm. You've been coming up with every excuse in the book to fight with me and that scares me. Scares the hell out of me, and if you don't want this relationship to go any further, just say so, dammit. Say so right now, and I promise you that I will move on. You know I've been hurt before, Trina. The last thing I want is to be hurt again."

Keith didn't wait for a response. He pushed his dick inside of me and started to rock my body with his. "I love you," he said in a whisper. "Can't you see that? What do I need to do to get you to see how much I really love you?"

A slow tear rolled down my cheek. Deep down, I knew I had been giving him a hard time. I knew that I kicked up an argument, and kept it going because I was afraid to move in with him. The last time I moved in with a man, he'd hurt me so badly. He abused me and controlled my every move. I was afraid of that happening again, but I didn't realize that this was Keith. He had been so good to me. I suspected that some of this stuff with Evelyn was done to upset me. I was sure that he hadn't had sex with her. He wasn't that kind of man. Shame on me for insisting that he was.

I reached out and wrapped my arms around his neck. Kissed him like it was going out of style. Rocked my body with his and apologized over and over again for my foolish behavior.

"I'm sorry. Please forgive me. I love you too, and I promise to never hurt you like she did. Your ex was a fool. I'm not, so whenever you're ready for me to move in with you, I will."

Keith wet my juicy lips with his. We continued to fuck on the car, not caring who saw us on the darkened parking lot. I wrapped my legs around his back, leaned back as he sucked my titties and ground with him until I could grind no more. Hell, yeah, we put on a scene, and when I released an orgasm, you'd better believe that plenty of people who looked on heard about it.

Chapter 12

Evelyn

When I received the selfie of Kayla and Cedric, I pursed my lips and tossed my phone on the couch. How foolish of her to send that crap to me, like I was supposed to jump for joy or call Cedric to see what was up. Now that I wasn't pregnant anymore, there wasn't much that he could do for me. Bryson had helped with my finances, so this thing with Kayla and Cedric really wasn't a big deal. That day, I sent Kayla a text message, congratulating her for finally coming to her damn senses. If I had some extra money, I'd have flowers delivered to her, but that trick wasn't even worth one rose.

Then there was ol' crybaby Trina. She was just as crazy as Kayla was. The more she clowned on Keith, the better my chances were at getting to him. Yeah, I was still kicking it with Bryson, but he was just my little plaything. We had fun

together, and the truth was, we couldn't stop
screwing each other. My first day at work, we
found ourselves in the bathroom stall getting
it on. Then, we went to the park for lunch and
started having sex in the car. Since Libby was
still on her trip, I invited him to my place. We
got busy in the shower, and then took our business to Keith's house the following day. Several
of their friends came over, and Bryson invited
me to come over. Like always, we played cards,
listened to music, and watched TV. Bryson took
me upstairs to one of the guestrooms and we
indulged ourselves. Keith walked in on us, too,
and Lord knows I wanted to ask him to join us.
But timing was everything. All I wanted was one
chance. Just one opportunity to be with him.
There was something about him that I couldn't
allow my best friend to keep all to herself. Maybe
if I suggested that the two of us do him together,
maybe she'd get on board. After all, she used to
be, or still is, bisexual.

It was three o'clock in the afternoon and work
was almost over. I was kind of bored, especially
since Bryson was out of the office and on one
of the construction sites. I got up to go to the
cafeteria for a soda and some chips. When I
got there, I saw three black women sitting at a
table gossiping. I could tell they were whispering

about me, because their eyes kept shifting in my direction. I could also hear some of what they were saying. I heard words like: whore, tramp, Bryson, diseases, and white bitch. They laughed, and when I snapped my head around, fake smiles were on display. I got my snacks and walked over to the table.

"Hi, ladies," I said with a smile. "And FYI, all of you are correct. I am a whore, I am fucking and sucking the hell out of Bryson's disease-infected dick, and he is still planning to marry the white bitch. That's after I get finished with him, so keep on paying attention. I'm sure you'll all have more to gossip about soon."

Their mouths hung wide open. I started to walk away and couldn't believe what one of the women had the audacity to ask me.

"Did you clean up his sperm shots in the restroom? That's just nasty, and next time y'all need to get a room."

"Next time, and trust me when I say there will be a next time, please opt to use another restroom when that one is being occupied."

I rolled my eyes and walked off. Some women were so petty and jealous. Just like my so-called BFF's were. I guess I couldn't call them my BFF's anymore, because we had gone way beyond that. Maybe my FFF's. Fake Fucking Friends who I just didn't care about anymore. That included Trina, but I needed her "friendship" in order to accomplish some things.

When I got back to my desk, I saw that I'd missed a call from Bryson. I called him back and he quickly answered his phone.

"What's the play for today?" I teased.

"Nothing. I called to tell you that I'm working late and won't be able to come over tonight. Maybe tomorrow."

"Awww, that's not good news. But tomorrow will just have to do. Maybe we can meet at Keith's house since the game is coming on. He has that big ol' television that you like to watch."

"I thought about that too, but Trina will be there. I think they're trying to patch things up, so I don't want to keep getting in the way. For now, it'll have to be your place. You know Libby kind of acting up, and I don't want to put you in the middle."

"Please don't. Confirm everything with me tomorrow."

"Will do, Miss Sexy. Be good."

"Never," I said then laughed.

Bryson laughed too and then hung up. I couldn't believe that Trina had weaseled her way back in with Keith. I definitely had to call her to see what was up with that. I called her, pretending as if I didn't know they were back together.

"Trina?" I said, as she spoke in a low tone.

"What?"

"Are you okay?"

"Not really, but whatever. What's up?"

"No, the question is what's up with you? I haven't heard from you in a few days. I thought we were good."

"We are good, Evelyn. I'm just trying to sort through some things right now."

"Things like what? If you need to talk, I'm listening."

"I know, but I get tired of running to you with my problems. I can't ever seem to get my footing when it comes to relationships. All this back-and-forth stuff with Keith is driving me crazy."

"Have you spoken to him? The last time I talked to you, things were kind of sketchy."

"They're still sketchy. We tried to reconcile. Had sex and everything. I told him I was going to move in with him, but then I found out that he's still been talking to his ex-girlfriend. She reached out to me last night. Told me everything. I am so done with men. How many chances do I have to give them to get it right?"

"Well, women have their issues too. Maybe it's just Keith. I told you before how sneaky he was, but you refused to listen. Why don't you just chill for a while, like me? Stop trying to force relationships on people who aren't ready."

"Maybe I do need to chill for a while. This is the last motherfucker I'm going to allow to hurt me. I've got to stop trusting people so much."

"I couldn't agree with you more. The way I see it, this is Keith's loss. You're a good person, Trina. If he didn't realize that, too bad."

"Kayla just said the same thing. I so wish the three of us could get together and go have some fun like we used to. Do you remember when we all went to Miami Beach together? We had so much fun. I swear those were the days."

Truthfully, I didn't have that much fun in Miami Beach with my BFF's, but if she insisted that we did, who was I to dispute it?

"Yes, those were the days. But things have changed and here we are."

"Right. But how did we get here is the question? We used to be soooo close, and our bond was unbreakable. But look at us now."

Sad, wasn't it? I had to admit that we did have some good times too. "Truthfully, we got here because of Kayla's selfishness and her thinking she was always better than us. I wouldn't have ever started sleeping with Cedric, if Kayla wouldn't have treated me like a nobody. As for us, we've had our issues too. But you already know how much I care about our friendship. It means a lot to me."

"You say that, Evelyn, but sometimes your actions don't show it. Where Kayla is concerned, no matter what, you never should have been sleeping with her husband. She may have been selfish, but that wasn't a reason for you to open your legs and get pregnant by Cedric."

"There you go taking her side again. I wish we would eliminate Kayla from our conversations. What's done is done. It makes no sense to keep harping on the past. Besides, she's supposed to be real happy now. She sent me a selfie of her and Cedric, holding their divorce papers. I don't know why she went there, but I guess you may know better than I do."

"That wasn't a bright idea, but whatever. I won't mention her name again, nor will I keep on bringing you my sob stories about Keith. I'm going away for a few days. Need some time to think, so I'm heading to an art show in L.A. this evening. I'll be gone for three days. When I get back, maybe we can hook up."

"Sounds good. Keep your head up, girl, and don't let no man stress you. Have a good time, and we'll hook up when you get back."

Trina and I left it there. I felt a little bad for her, but that's the way the boat rocks sometimes. Her news also had me thinking. If she wasn't going to be around for a few days, hmmmm.

I sat for a few minutes, pondering. Then I got up and went into Bryson's office. I closed the door and hurried over to his desk. I'd seen several keys in his drawer, but one key had a piece of tape on it that read Keith. I assumed it was a key to his house. I searched Bryson's desk, but the only thing I came across were a bunch of pens and pencils, notepads, and a few pictures of unattractive women. I tossed the pictures in the trash, especially the one of a woman who had a pudgy stomach and a tattoo between her legs. Yucky. When I lifted a camera, that was when I saw a silver key and one with Keith's name taped to it. I tucked the keys into my pocket and hurried to get back to my desk.

Five o'clock rolled around; I couldn't wait to get home. I showered, changed clothes, then sat back on my couch. For some reason, I was a little nervous about reaching out to Keith, so I picked up a Newport and lit it. I took a puff, and then whistled smoke into the air. Took another puff and did the same. Before I knew, the cigarette was almost finished. That was when I picked up my cell phone to call him. My pussy thumped a little from the sound of his sexy yet sad voice.

"I hope I didn't catch you at a bad time, but I wanted to ask you a few questions about Bryson, if you don't mind."

"You're timing is cool. I've been painting all day and need to take a break anyway. Shoot."

"Well, I'm not sure if you know this or not, but Bryson and I have been getting a little close lately. I'm finding myself feeling him, a lot, but I'm also feeling someone else too. Then there's the situation with him and Libby. I was at his place one day and she showed up. She was pretty distraught, and I felt terrible for hurting her like that. Bryson seems as if he cares for her, but a part of me feels as if I'm in the way. Do you think I should back off? Or do you think I should stop seeing him altogether and direct my attention to the other person I'm feeling?"

"First, I will say this to you. Libby and my brother have been together for a long time. Eventually, he's going to settle down, and if he does, it'll probably be with her. Then again, he's so hard to figure out. He is involved with several other women too. From what he's said to me, I'm sure you already know that, right?"

"Yes, I do. That doesn't bother me, as much as this thing with Libby does. To see her so upset like that really troubled me. I wouldn't wish the pain that she's going through on my worst enemy. A big part of me feels as if I'm contributing to her pain."

"In a sense, you are. But so are other people. If it's bothering you that much, back off. Chill for a while, and pursue the other person you're interested in. That's what I would do. At the end of the day, Bryson will be just fine."

"I think he would be too. I know his kind all too well. Now, in reference to the other guy, he's in a tricky situation as well. The woman who he likes is confused. She really doesn't know what she wants and she's a little drama queen. I think he's just about had it with her, but I'm not so sure. He's one of the nicest men that I've ever met, and I can't stop thinking about him. All I want is one night . . . one night with him and I would want no more."

Keith stayed silent for a moment. Then he cleared his throat. "One night to do what with him?"

"One night to have passionate sex with him. There is something in his eyes that says he wants me, but he's afraid. Afraid that what I intend to do to him will get back to his girlfriend. Thing is, it won't. My lips are sealed and I would take that secret to my grave. My question to you is, do you think I should pursue this man?"

Keith paused again. I heard his breathing increase then a sigh followed. "I don't know if he would risk losing everything for one night of passionate sex. You may have to offer him a little bit more than that."

"I would offer him anything he wanted. I'm feeling him that much, and if he wanted more, the sex could be viewed as a jumpstart."

"Anything?"

"Anything."

"I don't see any man rejecting your offer, but if the confused woman is a drama queen, shouldn't you be worried?"

"Women don't scare me. They never have. I always go for what I want, even though, sometimes, people tend to get hurt in the process. I like to deal with those situations as they come. They're always after the fact. After I've gotten what I wanted, and the other person has gotten what they wanted too."

"So, in other words, let the chips fall where they may."

"Exactly. Now, I'll ask again. Should I, or shouldn't I pursue him?"

Keith hesitated longer this time. "I . . . I think you should. Maybe you should go by his place tonight, around nine, and see what's up with him. If the door is unlocked, go to his bedroom where he'll probably be watching TV, since the drama queen who is causing him plenty of headaches will be out of town. Wear something real sexy to entice him and don't forget to bring condoms. You always want to stay strapped up, especially when you don't know what he's been into. I hope my advice helps, Evelyn. And let me know how everything turns out."

"You'll know soon."

I ended the call and hurried to call Trina, just to see where she was. She was already at the airport, waiting for her plane to depart.

"Have a safe trip," I said. "And be sure to call me when you arrive in L.A."

"Okay, I will. If I see a piece of art that you may like, I'll purchase it for you."

I laughed. "Don't waste your money. You know I prefer the cash over a painted picture any day."

"Right. Bye, girl. Holler later."

Much later, I thought.

I laid the phone on the table and tried to contain my enthusiasm for going to see Keith. I suspected that it wasn't going to be as simple as he'd made it, and I figured I'd had to put up a fuss to get him to give me what I wanted. I could tell so by the way he hesitated, but there was no question that by the time the night was over, Keith would be like putty in my hands.

If the man wanted sexy, I was going to give him sexy and then some. That consisted of me wearing nothing but my silky skin, underneath a coat. I changed into just that and left my place in a hurry.

As planned, when I arrived at Keith's house, the door was unlocked. I didn't even need the key I'd gotten from Bryson's office, but I still kept it. The downstairs was pretty dark. Upstairs was too, but I could see light from a television coming from his room. I sauntered up the stairs and heard soothing jazz music as well. He was apparently trying to set the mood, so I made my way to his doorway. I peeked inside and saw him sitting up in bed with a sheet covering him from the waist down. I knocked on the door and then walked inside. Keith picked up a watch from his nightstand.

"You're almost ten minutes late. I didn't think you were coming. I was about to fall asleep, because these shows on the television are boring."

"Then Evelyn to the rescue, right?"

I didn't want to waste any time with this. Keith appeared to be on board, and that was a good thing. His eyes locked on me as I removed the belt from my coat. When I peeled it away from my shoulders, I saw him suck in a deep breath. I stood before him, with no clothes on and ready to handle my business. Keith patted the spot next to him then cocked his head back.

"Come here," he said softly. "My brother said you were sexy as hell. I guess now I believe him."

I crawled on the bed like a courageous tiger. Moved face to face with him then leaned in for a kiss. This time, he didn't back away. He didn't reject me, and his mouth opened wide. I couldn't believe what a great kisser he was. No wonder Trina was hooked.

"Sweet lips," he said, holding the sides of my face. He lightly bit my lips a few times, and then backed away when the phone rang.

"Sweet pussy too," I replied. "Wait until you taste it."

The ringing phone interrupted us again.

"You may want to go answer that," I said. "Just in case it's you-know-who. The last thing you may want is her showing up here tonight."

Keith shrugged, but he took my advice. He snatched the sheet away from him. Lord have mercy on that body of his.

"I'll go get my phone, and why don't you run to the kitchen to get us some wine out the fridge?"

I really didn't want any wine, but since Keith was cooperating, what the hell? I went to the kitchen to get the wine, and then stopped by the bathroom to pee. I could hear Keith going off on somebody over the phone, but then his voice went silent. It was probably Trina.

Then again, she was on a plane to L.A. Keith's ex-girlfriend came to mind, so I hurried out of the bathroom to eavesdrop on the conversation.

I returned to the bedroom with the wine bottle and two glasses in my hand. Keith was back in bed, lying on his side with the sheet covering him. The television had been turned off, and his cell phone was on the nightstand, ringing again. This time, he ignored it and didn't say a word. I set the wine and glasses down then crawled on the bed next to him again. When I pulled the sheet away from him, that was when I got the shock of my life. I eased away from the gun that was aimed right at the center of my forehead, which was starting to build up a sheen of sweat. The look in Trina's eyes was deadly.

"Bitch," she said through gritted teeth. "You got five motherfucking seconds to get your coat back on and get the hell out of my man's house! And if you ever, I mean ever, come back here again, I swear to God that I will blow your damn brains out!"

Trina didn't look like she was bullshitting, so I didn't bother to respond. I kept my eyes on the gun that trembled in her hand and carefully eased back on the bed. I bent down to pick up my coat, but didn't bother to put it back on. I waved at her, and jetted down the stairs so fast that I almost fell and broke my neck. Keith awaited me at the door. His face looked like stone, as he held the door wide open. I was too embarrassed to say one word. After I ran outside, he slammed the door so hard that it shook the house. Apparently, he wasn't down with my plans after all.

Chapter 13

Kayla

Trina called to tell me about her and Keith's plan for Evelyn. She had me laughing my tail off. I couldn't believe how desperate Evelyn had gotten. Since Cedric was no longer around, I should've expected something like that from her.

"I always knew she was scantless, but when Keith told me about her trying to hook up with him before, I couldn't believe it. This last thing was his idea. He wanted to show me what was really going on behind my back. When she called to speak to him about coming over, I was right there listening."

"Girl, I'm convinced that Evelyn is crazy. She needs some serious help. No woman in her right mind could be foolish enough to go into her best friend's man's house with nothing on and try to seduce him. Does she really think she's got it going on like that? And what about Bryson? Did Keith tell him?"

"Nope. He said he wasn't going to say a word, because Evelyn was going to get her feelings hurt, again, messing around with him. She's always running after men, but she'd better be careful what she wishes for."

"I know that's right. Right away I could tell Bryson was no good. He started talking all that mess at the club that night, but all I did was smile and listen. I had fun, but the truth is, I need to take time out and see about me. I'm not pursuing any relationship, until I get my stuff over here in order and make sure Jacoby is on the right track. Something seems to be troubling him, but I can't put my finger on it. Maybe it has to do with the divorce, but I explained to him that it was something I truly had to do for myself."

"I totally get that. He'll understand one day why you did what you had to do. And before I forget, thank you for interfering in my relationship. I'm glad you called Keith to come to the club. We needed to settle things down and talk through our differences."

"I figured the two of you would. I only interfere when I feel as though I have to. I didn't want you to make the mistake of losing him. Have you moved in yet?"

"Yep. Moved in a few days ago. I'm feeling good about this, too. Now, what about you? Have you heard from Cedric, and when are you going to start looking for another place to stay? Staying in that hotel must be driving you nuts."

"It is, and I'm getting tired of the ongoing noise, too. I think I found a place near Chesterfield. The rent is ridiculous, but I love how the apartment is made."

"Apartment? You're moving into an apartment?"

"Yes. It's a three bedroom, but it's humongous. It's perfect for me and Jacoby. We really don't need anything bigger than that."

"What about the house? Did Cedric put it up for sale yet?"

"He said he was going to next week. We've talked here and there, but more so about Jacoby and our finances. Cedric set me out. I must say that I'm very appreciative of the money we agreed upon in our divorce settlement."

"That's good. Seems like everything is working out for everybody, with the exception of Evelyn. Maybe she'll come to her senses and start doing the right thing. If she does, I'll never know about it because she would be too embarrassed to ever contact me again."

"Tuh, don't believe that for one minute. Sooner or later, you'll get a call. She'll be begging and pleading for you to forgive her. And I know you, Trina. You probably will."

Trina denied it, but among the three of us, she was the one with the forgiving heart. To a certain extent, I was too. But it would be very, very difficult for me to ever forgive Evelyn.

We talked for a little while longer, but since I was supposed to meet Jacoby at the apartment complex so he could see it, I had to let Trina go. I then called Jacoby, but he didn't answer his phone. I drove to Adrianne's house to see if he was there. He was, and I found the two of them outside arguing. I didn't like how heated the conversation between them seemed, so I got out of the car to go break it up. Jacoby was way too aggressive. I yelled for him to back away from Adrianne.

"Jacoby," I shouted again. "Didn't you hear me?"

He backed away with a mean mug on his face. Adrianne had been crying. This whole scene was kind of shocking to me because I thought things had been going well for them.

"Anybody want to tell me what's going on here?" I said.

"Tell her," Adrianne shouted. "Now is the time to tell her!"

Jacoby narrowed his eyes at her and shot daggers. "Shut up! Stay out of this, Adrianne, it's none of your business!"

I couldn't express how shocked I was. I put my hand on my hip and frowned. "Tell me what? Would somebody please tell me so that we can talk about whatever it is in a sensible way?"

"It's nothing, Mama. If you want to go see this apartment, let's go."

"If this is about the apartment, please let me know. I'll accept if you don't want to live with me, and you prefer to live with Cedric. We will always be a family, and you are welcome—"

"Tell her now," Adrianne shouted again. "She needs to know the truth!"

This was driving me nuts. I turned to Jacoby and let him have it. "The truth about what," I yelled. "What secret are you keeping from me?"

Jacoby had the look of fire in his eyes. He turned to walk away, but I ran after him. "Is she pregnant? Is that what you want to tell me? I told you about having all this sex, Jacoby, and the least you could've done was protect yourself. You haven't even graduated from high school yet and—"

"No," Adrianne said. "I'm not pregnant. And if you don't tell her what you did, I'm going to tell her myself."

I was floored when Jacoby reached out and grabbed Adrianne's face. He squeezed it tight and held his hand over her mouth. This time, I yanked him away from her and pushed him back. I pointed my finger near his face and gritted my teeth.

"No son of mine will ever put his hands on a woman like that! What in the hell is wrong with you? Who are you, Jacoby, and what in the hell are you keeping from me?"

Adrianne stepped back and blurted out the secret. "He paid Paula Daniels to kill Cedric. I begged him not to do it, but Jacoby wouldn't listen. We don't know why she hasn't said anything about it, but he's been so afraid that she's going to tell someone."

I stood as if cement had been poured over me. I couldn't believe what Adrianne had said. Things were just starting to look up for us, but now this.

"You did what?" I said to Jacoby. "Why . . . how . . . what made you do something so stupid? You didn't have to involve yourself in this mess, Jacoby. Why did you want your father dead?"

Jacoby stood with a frightened look on his face. Finally, he started to speak up. "I didn't want him dead. Well, at first I did, but then I changed my mind. I knew how much Paula despised him, and all she needed was a little push. I offered her the money and she said she would do it. But then things kinds of settled down at our house, and when I went back to see her, she said the plan was already in motion and that I couldn't renege." Jacoby paused to take a deep breath. He placed his hands behind his head then turned around to face the other direction. Shame was written all over his face.

"I had already given her the money. She wouldn't give it back and she told me to get out. Then, Cedric was shot. I knew she did it, but I don't know if she's planning to tell the police about my involvement. If she does, they're not going to believe that I tried to stop her. Nobody will believe me. That was why I didn't want to say anything. I wanted to tell you the truth, as well as Cedric. But I couldn't. I just couldn't do it." Jacoby broke down in tears. He leaned against his car and cried like a baby.

I was numb about the whole thing, but this was still my son. I regretted not taking action sooner, regarding my marriage. Jacoby felt as if he had to step in and handle things for me. Thus far, Paula hadn't said anything. She pleaded guilty to the attempted murder charge and so be it. If she ever came back and tried to tell on Jacoby, we'd deny it. Even if she had evidence, we'd get one of the best lawyers in St. Louis to fight the case. But the person I was worried about was Cedric. What if he ever found out the real deal? Was it in my best interest to tell him, or should I leave well enough alone? I suspected what Jacoby's answer would be, when I suggested that we go see Cedric.

"We need to talk to him about this," I said while rocking Jacoby in my arms.

"Noooo," he cried out. "Please don't tell him, Mama. I beg you not to tell him. I know Cedric. He will turn me in. He will make me pay for this, and I don't want to go to jail."

Just the thought of Jacoby doing any time in jail pained me. Jail wasn't for my son. I couldn't let that happen, and as a matter of fact, I wouldn't let it happen. This was yet another secret that I'd have to keep to myself. Meanwhile, I had to hope and pray that this never got back to Cedric.

Later that day, I went to the new apartment complex to pay my first month's rent and security deposit. The quicker I got Jacoby away from Cedric the better. Jacoby had been through so much. When Adrianne told me that he'd contemplated suicide over this situation, I cried my heart out. Not my son. My focus was now on him. I didn't have time for anything else. He had two more years left of school, was a very bright student, and had always done well. For the past several months, he'd been consumed with my mess. Consumed with trying to keep this family together. I wanted to tell Cedric just that, but unlike me, he wouldn't understand. He would turn things around and make Jacoby seem like a murderer. He would disown him. Say that he was no good because Arnez's blood was the blood running through Jacoby's body, not his. Cedric would make our lives a living hell, and that was without a shadow of doubt.

After I left the rental office, I went to Cedric's house. Jacoby was supposed to meet me there, so we could start gathering his things and putting them in boxes. He wasn't there yet, so I called his cell phone. He told me that he was en route. I used my key to unlock the door, and the second I walked inside, Cedric was right there. He looked even better than he did before, and this time he was dressed in one of his tailored business suits.

"Why didn't you tell me?" he rushed to say.

My heart raced, and I moved my head from side to side. "I . . . Didn't tell you what?"

"You could have told me, and shame on you for not saying one word."

Seriousness was in his eyes. Then all of a sudden he laughed. He patted my shoulder and walked over to the door to close it. "Why didn't you say anything about our anniversary? Did you forget that it was today or what? You should be ashamed of yourself, if you forgot. Then again, I won't hold it against you. I forgot too, right until the second you walked through that door."

I sucked in a deep, long breath and sighed from relief. "Uh, yeah, sorry but I forgot too. And are you sure that today is our anniversary? I thought it was a week from today."

Cedric shook his head and strutted toward his office. I followed. He sat in his chair and looked at the calendar on his desk.

"Sorry, baby. It's today. You got it wrong, and like always, I'm right."

"Okay then, Mr. Right. Where have you been? You dressed all nice, and I must say that you look awfully handsome."

Cedric smiled and leaned back in his chair. He propped his feet on the desk and placed his hands behind his head. His scruffy beard had been shaved and his skin glowed.

"I had a meeting with my business partners today, and I also met with my attorney. You did good with keeping up the payments on things, and I appreciate your efforts. All I can say is I'm glad to be back. Feeling good and ready to make some big moves. The house goes on the market tomorrow, but just so you know, when it sells, every dime goes in my pocket. Now, if you need any of this furniture, let me know. That way, I won't sell it."

"I'm good. I kind of want all new stuff."

"Well, you damn sure have enough money to buy all new stuff. And then some, Miss Husband-made Millionaire."

"Ooo, look at you. You sound bitter. Are you?"

"Not at all. There's more where that came from, and if things go accordingly, there will be way more. So, uh, getting back to our anniversary. Since you're here, would you like to throw some pussy my way and see if I'll catch it?"

Just then, we heard the front door open. I figured it was Jacoby, and it was confirmed when he came into Cedric's office. Jacoby barely wanted to look at him. His head hung low and he spoke in a soft voice to both of us.

"What's up with you, man?" Cedric said. "Looks like you got girl problems."

"Yeah, something like that," Jacoby said with a fake smile. "You know how it is."

"Hell, yeah, I know how it is. But don't sweat the small stuff, and always focus on bigger things. I got a lot to teach you, son, especially when it comes to women. Never let them get you down, and always stay up. You hear me?"

Jacoby nodded.

"Go ahead to your room and start getting some of your things," I said. "I have the key to the apartment, so we can move some of your stuff in tonight."

Jacoby left the room and did what he was told.

"Tell me again," Cedric said, sitting up straight. "Where is this apartment again?"

"It's in Chesterfield. Close by the Missouri River, got three bedrooms, two and a half baths, two fireplaces, a loft area, and a chef's kitchen. The clubhouse is off the chain, too. I can't wait for you to see it."

"To hell with seeing it. Do I get a key?"

"I'm afraid not, Cedric. How many times am I going to have to tell you that I'm your ex-wife? We don't get down like that anymore."

"Exes still be fucking each other, so don't stand there like those legs are locked down because we're not married anymore. If you want to keep holding out on me, don't be mad at me for going elsewhere. I'm starting to feel an urge."

"Have all the urges you want, just don't mosey your tail over to you-know-who's place. She's got enough trouble on her hands, and the last person she needs to drop back in is you."

"Who are you talking about? Evelyn?"

"Yes. Evelyn."

Cedric winced and blew me off. "Whatever. Evelyn is old news. Whatever trouble she's found herself in, it doesn't surprise me."

I couldn't help but to share what had happened between Evelyn, Trina, and Keith. Every chance I got, I wanted to make sure she looked bad through his eyes. I also wanted him to say that he had regrets about their relationship, but thus far, he hadn't said it. He sat in disbelief as I spoke. Couldn't stop shaking his head and cracking up. Then he slapped his leg and rubbed his chin.

"She that gotdamn trifling where she trying to fuck two brothers? They must have some money. Otherwise, I can't see her going out like that."

"Of course they do, but even if they didn't, she probably would have gone there. Trina is so pissed. We're to the point where we seriously believe Evelyn needs to see a psychiatrist."

"Yeah, maybe so."

He didn't seem too interested in talking about Evelyn, so I told Cedric that I was getting ready to go help Jacoby pack up some of his things. He stopped me at the door.

"When the two of you get settled into the apartment, do me a favor and have a long talk with our son. He's been a little off lately, and I'm worried about him. It could be about something with Adrianne, but usually, Jacoby don't let girl problems get to him like that. I think there's something else."

I started to bite my nails. "So . . . something else like what? What do you think is bothering him?"

"Not sure. He hasn't been right since I was shot. Maybe seeing me like that has done something to him. After you talk to him, I will. Okay?"

"Sure. I'll keep you posted on how the conversation goes. Meanwhile, happy anniversary, and please don't do anything that I wouldn't do."

Cedric held out his hands. "The sky is the limit. The last time I checked, I'm a free man. Unfortunately, since you're not interested anymore, I may be prompted to take another woman out to dinner and make love to her on our anniversary. Remember, I told you about my urge."

I threw my hand back at Cedric and left his office. At this point, I guess I didn't care who he spent his time with, as long as it wasn't Evelyn.

Jacoby and I spent the next few hours packing up some of his things. During that time, Cedric said he was going somewhere and left. Jacoby and I discussed, again, how all of this came about and how to move forward. He sat on the bed in his bedroom, shaking his head while I sat next to him.

"I know you want to say something to him, Mama, but you know your husband better than I do. My dad can be a monster when he wants to be, and nobody wants to find out they've been betrayed."

"I do want to tell him, but more than anything, I want to protect you. I definitely know how Cedric is; I've lived with him for most of my life. More than anything, I'm glad you got all of this off your chest. I can only imagine how keeping this inside has made you feel, but I wish you would have come to me so I could help you get through this."

"Trust me when I say I wanted to. Adrianne definitely wanted me to, but I didn't know how you would feel about me paying Paula to do something so horrific. At the time, my head wasn't on straight. I was so upset with my dad, and when I tried to reach out to him about how I felt one day, my timing couldn't have been more off. I saw him in a parking garage with Paula, doing some crazy stuff that no married man should be doing."

I could only imagine what Cedric was doing. The thought made me sick to my stomach. And then for Jacoby to witness it was awful.

"I don't need details, and reaching out to him was all you could do. You were not thinking straight, and I assume you used the money in your savings to pay Paula, didn't you?"

"Every dime of it. When I asked for it back, she laughed at me. I had no idea what kind of woman she really was, until I witnessed that evil look in her eyes. She hated Cedric with a passion. She was obsessed with him, but I can honestly say he created that monster."

He'd created several other monsters too, but I wasn't trying to go there right now with Evelyn. Jacoby and I finished packing, and a few hours later, we were on our way to our new apartment, ready for a new beginning. His secret was safe with me, and I intended to do whatever I had to do to protect my son.

Chapter 14

Evelyn

My feelings were a little bruised about what had happened, but oh well. You win some and you lose some. Trina had Keith's ol' weak self wrapped around her finger. For him to agree to do something so ridiculous was stupid on his part. I bet he was still thinking about that kiss, though. I tore up those lips. How could he ever forget about the sweet taste of my tongue?

The one thing that I was worried about was Keith telling Bryson about what had happened. For starters, I didn't want him to be so upset about it that I'd lose my job. I kind of liked where I worked, and it did bring in a little money to help me pay some bills. Then, I didn't want Bryson feeling as if I'd betrayed him. He'd been kicking me out every now and then. Not just sexually either. I never had to pay for dinner, never had to pay for drinks, and he even gave me some money to buy a purse that I had to have when browsing the mall with him the other day.

So in a nutshell, losing him would be a setback for me, especially since he was the only person I could really chill with and carry on a decent conversation with. I wasn't ready to go see what was up with Cedric yet, and the more I'd thought about it, I was skeptical about traveling back down memory lane with him. The last conversation we'd had didn't go so well. I left his house that day plotting my next move because he wouldn't allow me to move in with him. He rejected that move, but he left me with a little hope about him taking care of the baby. Now that there was no baby, I wasn't so sure if he'd welcome me back with open arms. He hadn't called to say anything to me, and I wondered if Trina had told Kayla about the abortion, and if she'd told Cedric. I was almost positive that she'd mentioned it to him.

Then again, maybe not because I'd been left out of everything when it came to those two. It was a wrap in regard to my friendship with them. I didn't suspect that we would ever be able to have the bond we all shared, and at this point, all the damage had won the battle. So be it.

I'd been off work for about an hour. Bryson said that he was working late, but he promised to call when he got home. I wasted time by going to the grocery store and then I stopped at Walmart to pick up a few cleaning items. By the time I was done with that, it was almost eight o'clock. I still hadn't heard from Bryson, and to be honest, I was kind of getting a little irritated with him for telling me one thing, yet doing another. Like saying that he would call me. Sometimes, he never did. I wouldn't even stress him about it the next day at work, and he never provided an explanation as to why he hadn't called.

Well tonight, I wasn't having it. I left a message on his voice mail, telling him that if he didn't show up, I was going to stop by his place. I didn't see it as popping up, especially if I told him I was coming through. If anything, I figured that my threat would, at least, encourage him to call. It didn't. By ten o'clock, I still hadn't heard from him. I grabbed my keys off the counter, reached for my jacket, and threw it over my shoulder. Bryson's condo was about forty minutes away from my place. It wasn't long before I parked my car on the parking lot and prepared myself to go to his door. I saw his car, so I assumed he was home. But when I called his cell phone, yet again, he didn't answer.

With my high heels on, I strutted to his door and knocked. No answer. Rang the doorbell;

nothing. If he was inside with someone else, the least he could do was come to the door and tell me. For whatever reason, he refused to do that. So, what I did was knock again. I put my ear to the door and heard loud music coming from somewhere. I wasn't sure if the music was coming from inside of his condo, but the music could have been his reason for not answering the door.

All of a sudden, something hit me. When I looked for Keith's key in the drawer, there was another key there as well. I'd taken both keys, and I wondered if that key was the one to unlock Bryson's door. I rummaged through my purse and finally found the key dropped inside of it. I slid the key in the lock, but unfortunately it wouldn't turn. That was when I realized that it was turned the wrong way. I turned it the other way, and yes, I was in business. The key turned and the door popped open. I pushed on it, causing it to squeak. Once I was inside, the music was louder. I also heard grunts, and that was when I figured that, maybe, this was a bad idea.

Still, I tiptoed my way forward. I saw a pair of lace panties in the middle of the floor. A bra was tossed on the couch, her shoes were right near the door, and the closer I got to it, I could hear

Bryson's grunts more than I could hear hers. It was so apparent that she was putting it on him. So much so that it sounded like he was crying. He whimpered like a bitch, and the sound of naked, sweaty bodies slapping together got louder and louder. My heels sank in the plush carpet as I reached the door, and when I turned in the doorway, I got a shock that felt like electricity had ripped through me. My legs weakened, my stomach tightened, and I covered my mouth so I wouldn't throw up. My eyes witnessed Bryson bending over the bed with a tranny behind him. The tranny was wearing Bryson out. His grunts were louder than the music in the room. I removed my hand from my mouth, refusing to walk away and hold my peace.

"You nasty, stank-ass motherfucker," I shouted. "How dare you not call me because of this!"

Both of their heads snapped to the side. The tranny looked like a beautiful black woman with nice breasts and a round, tight ass. Thing was, she/he had a dick. A big one, too, which she/he eased out of Bryson who had already jumped away from the tranny like she/he was contagious.

"What are you doing here?" he yelled at me.

"No. The question is what in the hell are you doing? I mean, really, Bryson. Is this how you're doing it?"

Embarrassment, as well as shame, covered Bryson's face. He hurried into his sweatpants and ordered the tranny to get on his/her clothes.

"You do not have to tell Miss Thing to leave on my account," I said. "I'm out of here, sweetheart. My eyes have witnessed enough."

I got the hell out of there. My body felt grimy as hell. I couldn't help but to think about all of the sex Bryson and I had had, and about all of the things that I allowed him to do to me. I had flashbacks of how he would touch me, and about how he requested that I touch him. He loved to have anal sex, and all of his little nasty ways now made sense. I definitely had no problem with gay or bisexual men, but I damn sure had a problem with the down-low motherfuckers who kept this kind of shit a secret.

I ran to my car and drove like a bat out of hell to get home. When I did, I stripped my clothes off and put the hot water in the shower on blast. I scrubbed my body with a sponge, but that felt like it wasn't working for me. What I needed was a Brillo pad, but unfortunately I didn't have any. I used the last one I had to clean the oven last week. I continued with the sponge and scalding hot water. My skin had turned red and my pussy couldn't get any cleaner. I finally turned off the water, and that was when I heard someone buzzing me from downstairs. I left the bathroom and turned on the monitor. The face that I saw was Bryson's.

"Say," he said in a whisper. "Why you leave so fast? I thought you wanted to see me."

"Oh, I saw you, but forget it. We have nothing else to talk about. I assure you that you never have to worry about me again. I will bring your key to the office tomorrow, and if you feel a need to have me fired, please do."

"I would never do that," he said, trying to smooth talk his way inside. That may have worked for Cedric, but damn sure not for him. "We don't even have to get down like that, do we? Why don't you buzz me in? I got a feeling that you're upset, and I need to provide you with an explanation about what you saw."

"Look, I don't need an explanation. Just go home, Bryson, and pretend that none of this ever happened."

"Can't do that right now. Besides, I don't want you to share what you saw tonight with anyone. If you do, that could swing a lot of heat my way, if you know what I mean."

All of a sudden, the sound of ca-ching went off in my head. I wanted to know what Bryson would be willing to pay for me to keep his dirty little secret. I had a feeling that it wouldn't be pennies. With that taken into consideration, I buzzed him in. The door was already opened for him to come inside, and when he did, I was sitting on the couch with my robe on. Another Newport was in my hand, and after I flicked ashes in the ashtray, I spoke up before he did.

"I don't want no explanation, I don't want any excuses, nor do I ever want you to touch me again. I am so disappointed in you, Bryson. How could a man as fine and masculine as you are holler louder than a bitch? I guess that's totally irrelevant right now; and the only question I need to be asking you is how much?"

"How much what?" he said with an attitude. He refused to take a seat, probably because his ass was still hurting from being bumped so hard.

I returned the attitude and snapped my head to the side. "How much are you going to pay me to keep my mouth shut?"

Bryson blew me off. He waved his hand and pursed his lips. The real bitch in him was starting to show. "I'm not paying you jack. You are not going to blackmail me, and if you tell anyone about what you saw tonight, they won't believe you. They'll think you're out of your mind, as plenty of people already think that you are. So rethink your plan, baby, or else."

I had to laugh at this fool. "How you gon' stand your greasy ass in here, trying to call the shots? They may not believe what I say, but they will believe me when I show them pictures that I took with my phone. You didn't see me take them because you were too busy getting got. I'm sure you don't want anyone to see you like that, especially not anyone at work, or your parents, and, uh, damn sure not Keith. He doesn't know about this, does he?"

I seemed to have Bryson's attention, even though I lied about the pictures. I wish I had taken some, but at the time, I was too in shock to even think straight.

Bryson walked slowly over to the couch and sat down. He rubbed his waves then cleared mucus from his throat.

"No," he said in a calmer tone. "Nobody knows. I've been hiding this for a very long time. I love women, no doubt, but I like men too. It's been that way since I was in high school, but I was afraid to tell my parents. Didn't want to tell my brother because I wasn't sure how he would feel about me. So please don't tell anyone about this. When I'm ready, I will say something. I'm just not ready yet."

I sat back and crossed my legs. "That was a tear-jerking little story there, Bryson, and

I have no problem keeping your secret. But it's going to cost you. You want to know why? Because you shouldn't have never put your dick inside of me, knowing that you also have a thing for men. If anything, you should have come clean about being bisexual and given me a chance to decide if I wanted to fuck with you. This down-low shit is a dangerous game to play. I hope to God that Libby knows what you're up to, and I guess that explains why you refused to settle down and marry her. At least you haven't been stupid enough to go that far."

"I haven't told her the truth yet, but one day I will. Then maybe she'll figure it out, since I'm refusing to marry her. Either way, I need to know that you're going to keep your mouth shut. I need to know your price, and if I give you any money, Evelyn, I don't want you reneging on me and putting my business out there. You have no idea how damaging something like this could be to me."

"If the price is right, I won't say a word. That price is a hundred thousand dollars. That's what it will take for me to keep my mouth shut."

"At that price, I may as well kill you then. I don't have that kind of money."

"Yes, you do. I saw the bank statements in your files. And if you don't have it, your parents do. Keith definitely has it, and all you have to do is ask him to sell one or two of those exquisite paintings in his studio. That's how you can get it and then some. As for killing me, don't bother. The word about you will still spread, because a good friend of mine already has those photos in her possession. She knows exactly what to do with them, if something happens to me. And we both know that, social media comes in handy when you need to use it to spread the word."

Bryson knew his hands were tied. He sat there and couldn't say shit. When he did open his mouth, he said exactly what I wanted to hear. I'd have the money by tomorrow. Certainly, that was good enough for me.

The next day, I walked into the office as if last night had never happened. I smiled at Bryson and he smiled back at me. He came over to my desk around noon, telling me that the money had been deposited into my account. I checked, and sure enough, sister girl was out of the negative. I was very happy about that. So happy that I wanted to go holler at an old friend of mine, so we could both celebrate our wealth. Hopefully, Cedric wouldn't refuse to see me.

Having a slew of money in my bank account caused me to pack it up and leave. My first stop was at the bank, where I withdrew several thousands of dollars to catch up on my bills. I prepaid my landlord three month's rent then I headed to the mall to purchase a pair of shoes and a pantsuit that I wanted. After that, I went to find a special gift for a dear friend of mine. Since I was going to stop by, it didn't make sense for me to stop by empty-handed.

I left the mall with several bags in my hands. Tossed them on the back seat, and then I made my way to Cedric's house. Upon arrival, the first thing I did was scope out the place to make sure Kayla's crazy self was nowhere around. I wasn't in the mood for another one of her slaps. My day had been on point, thus far, and I expected for it to get better.

Kayla's car was nowhere in sight and neither was Jacoby's. Cedric's BMW was parked in the driveway, and I was surprised to see a HOUSE FOR SALE sign in the yard. I figured that after the divorce was finalized, neither Cedric or Kayla would want to live in that house, especially since Cedric had almost been murdered in it. Something about that seemed creepy.

I was kind of excited about seeing Cedric, so I reached for his gift on the back seat and strutted to the front door. I rang the doorbell, and a few minutes later, Cedric opened the door. He looked fabulous and very clean cut in his business attire. I could always smell the dollars blowing in the air. His face, though, was without a smile. He looked me up and down, and hadn't invited me in yet.

The gift was behind my back, so I brought it forth to give it to him.

"Hello, handsome," I said. "I was at the mall today and I thought about you. I've been meaning to stop by and check on you, but time got away from me. Then I heard through the grapevine that you were putting your house up for sale. I'm very interested in purchasing it, but first, I kind of need for you to show me around. May I come in?"

Cedric stood for a moment, staring at me as if I had shit on my face. He then opened the door wider to let me inside. I tried to give him the gift again, but he wouldn't take it.

"Aww, Cedric, don't be so mean to me," I teased. "At least look at it. We both have good taste and creative minds. I'm sure you'll like it."

I forced the package his way again. This time, he snatched it from my hand and tore the shiny wrapping paper away from the box. When he opened it, inside was a protection kit that included Mace, a small pocket knife, and handcuffs.

I smiled at him and explained my nice gesture. "I thought those items may come in handy the next time any woman tries to come in your house and kill you. If you had those items in your possession, you could have sprayed that whore with Mace, stabbed her, and then handcuffed her until the police got here."

Cedric wet his lips with his tongue. He narrowed his eyes to look at the items then nodded. The next thing I knew, he reached out for my hair and pulled it tight. He then used his foot to trip me. I hit the marble floor in the foyer so hard that my ass hurt.

"Damn!" I shouted. "What in the hell did I say that was so wrong?"

Cedric flipped me on my stomach and pressed his knee into my back, damn near cracking it. He pulled my arms behind me and locked the cuffs on my wrists. I struggled to stop him, but to no avail. The cuffs were locked so tight that it felt as if they were cutting my wrists. While I was face down, he pulled my hair back to lift my head. He put the knife close to my neck and spoke through gritted teeth.

"Thanks for the bullshit gift. I'm glad that I could put it to good use. Let this be a warning to you that I'm not some motherfucking toy you can play with. I'm a changed man, and

I promise you that I am nothing like I was before. You don't want to fuck with me, and to be clear, I don't have time for bitches like you. You couldn't afford to live here, so take yo' ass back to that rattrap you live in. I never want to see your face again. Got it?"

Well damn. Since when did I manage to get on his bad side? I didn't respond quick enough to his "got it" question, so he dropped the knife and slammed my head on the marble foyer, face first. I heard my teeth crack and my lip felt numb. I also tasted blood stirring in my mouth, and I could feel it dripping down my chin. This was a clear sign that his ass wasn't playing with me. I nodded to answer his question, but that wasn't good enough for him.

"Speak up, tramp! I can't hear you. You're not allowed to come here, call me, nothing . . . ever again! Do you understand?"

The loudness of his voice caused my ears to ring. I quickly answered before he slammed my face again.

"Yes," I cried out with tears rolling down my face. "I do understand."

"Good!"

Cedric lifted me off the floor and escorted me over to the front door. He opened it, and used the key to remove the cuffs. As I massaged my wrists, he shoved me outside. I fell on the porch, scraping my knees. While rubbing them, he threw the wrapping paper, box, and contents at me. I ducked to avoid the flying can of Mace. After that, he slammed the door and locked it.

Shit was getting a little rough for me. My good day had turned bad. And when I got in the car to look at my mouth in the rearview mirror, it wasn't a pretty sight. My mouth was bloody and my front tooth dangled. It hurt, too, so instead of going back to the mall to shop, I made my way to the dentist and thought about ways to make Cedric pay for this. He was out of control. He didn't appear to be the man that he was before. Something about him was different. Maybe, just maybe, it was in my best interest to leave his ass alone. Or, at least, until he shook off some of that madness.

Chapter 15

Trina

Keith and I were back on track. Moving in with him was the best thing I could've done. Just yesterday, I cleared out my entire apartment and turned in my keys. I called Kayla to see if she would come help me, considering that she had lived with me for a while too. She said that she was busy. She'd been acting kind of funny lately. I asked if something was wrong, but she insisted that she didn't want to discuss it. Good, because like she had mentioned to me, I got tired of hearing about the negativity too. Maybe it was a good thing that she was keeping whatever it was that was bothering her to herself.

I came to the conclusion that the reason she didn't have time to help me with my apartment was because she was moving into hers. I hadn't seen it yet, but she told me how fabulous it was. I hoped to see it soon.

Keith had gone to the studio on Delmar to do some work. There were more supplies there to work with. We'd been spending so much time in this house, he needed to get out. I wasn't trying to keep him cooped up in here, but it was nice to wake up with a sexy, fine man lying next to me. Especially one who was great at lovemaking and who appreciated having sex quite often.

While he was gone, I started to clean up. The house had gotten kind of messy since I'd been here. I cleaned the bathrooms, washed the dishes, and did the laundry. As I sat in the living room folding clothes and watching TV, I looked through the huge picture window and saw Evelyn parking her car. I couldn't believe that she had the nerve to show her face over here again. I guess she thought Keith was here alone, but unfortunately for her, he wasn't.

Seething with anger, I stormed to the front door and swung it open before she even made it up the stairs.

"Really, Evelyn? You must be insane. Either that or I guess you don't believe I'm capable of stopping you with that gun that was introduced to you the last time you were here."

Evelyn slowed her pace, and she didn't reply. She paced her way up to me with sadness written all over her face. Tears welled in her eyes. Almost immediately, I saw her bruised, puffy lips; and a deep cut was on her lip, too. She threw her arms around me and dropped her head on my shoulder. She started to cry and could barely catch her breath as she tried to speak.

"I'm so, so sorry about what I did to you. Pleeese forgive me, Trina. I need for you to forgive me because I don't have nobody in my corner."

I pursed my lips, unable to sympathize with her. I didn't even bother to hug her back, but I intended to offer her some comforting words. I backed away from her tight embrace and looked at her disheveled appearance that I hadn't seen before. Her clothes were slouchy, bags were underneath her eyes, her hair was frizzy, and her skin appeared very pale. Not to mention, again, her swollen lips.

"Come into the living room and sit down. You always have someone in your corner. I don't have to remind you who He is."

"God don't help people like me. I don't know what's gotten into me. Ever since I lost my friendship with you and Kayla, things in my life haven't been right. My life has been going downhill, and I don't know what to do to stop it from sliding."

Evelyn fell back on the couch, tucking her leg underneath her. I reached for some tissue and gave it to her before taking a seat. She wiped her nose and dabbed her teary eyes. I wasn't going to respond to her comment about our friendship yet.

"What happened to your lip?" I asked. "Did you get into a fight with someone or did you and Kayla have another conversation?"

"No, I haven't seen her. Cedric did this to me. I stopped by his house the other day to give him a gift and to see how he was doing. He went crazy on me. Started punching me, and he knocked me on the floor. Took his fist and punched me in the face, and then he pounded my head on the floor. He knocked out my tooth, and I had to go to the dentist to get a tooth implant."

Evelyn was known for exaggerating. She grinned to show me her new tooth. I saw that the inside of her mouth was swollen and bruised. I frowned from how nasty it looked. A huge part of me didn't believe her, though. For her to say that Cedric had done all of that to her was a bit much. A dog he was, but an abusive man he wasn't.

"I don't know if he did that to you or not, but why would you go over there? After all that has happened, why don't you leave Cedric alone and be done with it?"

More tears fell from Evelyn's eyes. She wiped them then crumbled the tissue in her hand. I got up to get her some more tissue then sat back down to listen.

"Believe me, I tried to stay away from him, but I got lonely. There was a time when I could always reach out to you or Kayla, but you already know where we stand. With that in mind, I ran to Cedric for friendship and conversation. I thought we were still cool, and I don't understand what I did to make him hate me so much. Maybe the abortion upset him."

I surely didn't want to hurt her feelings. "I doubt that, and please forgive me because I'm still having a hard time believing all of this. You are so good at fabricating stories and embellishing them, Evelyn. I don't know what to believe. I promise you, though, that I won't get caught up in your games again."

Evelyn closed her eyes and moved her head from side to side. "I know I've been a terrible friend, and I've lied a lot in the past, too." She opened her eyes and looked at me. "But I'm not lying about what Cedric did to me. I swear to you that I'm not lying."

She pulled out her cell phone and dialed out. Afterward, she placed the phone between us and hit the speaker button. I heard a phone ringing. Seconds later Cedric answered. I guess knowing who the caller was, he tore into her right away.

"Didn't I tell you not to reach out to me again? I guess that ass kicking you got wasn't enough! If—"

Evelyn hit the end button and looked at me with more sadness. "See? I told you he beat me."

Damn. Why did I feel so bad for her? I tried my best not to let her know it. "He never should have put his hands on you. Maybe you need to press charges against him."

"I'm afraid to. He threatened me and said that he'd tell the police that I came over there to kill him, especially since this incident took place at his house. Considering what had happened with Paula, he assured me that the police would believe him. I just don't want any more trouble."

"Then stay away from there. If you needed companionship, friendship, or a conversation, why didn't you contact Bryson? Aren't you still kicking it with him? If not, what happened to y'all's relationship?"

Evelyn looked down and shook her head. She fumbled with the tissue then blew her nose again. This time, she stood and walked over to the picture window to look outside.

"I'll tell you what happened, but you have to promise me that you won't say anything to Keith. Is he here?"

"No, he's not. I can't promise you that I'll be keeping any secrets from him, though. We're striving to have a trustworthy and honest relationship."

"I get that, but this is something that you can't tell him. If you do, it will hurt him, and it could hurt me too. It involves Bryson and it's really, really bad. As for the two of us, I am so over him. It pains me to be around him every day at work, and I'm thinking about quitting."

Whatever it was sounded pretty darn juicy. I wasn't sure if I would tell Keith, especially if it was something that would hurt him. Regardless, I told Evelyn that I wouldn't say a word, just to get her to spill the beans.

"Promise me," she said, walking away from the window. "You have to promise me that you won't say anything. If you do, Bryson may hurt me even worse than Cedric did."

I was eager to hear what was up. "Okay, I promise. I won't say a word to Keith or anyone else."

Evelyn sat back down and went into great details about what she discovered with Bryson. The whole time she spoke, my eyes were bugged and my mouth was stuck wide open. When Evelyn was done, I flat out told her that she was a damn liar. That was when she told me about the money and showed me the deposit into her bank account.

"He begged me not to say a word to anyone. I don't even know if I should have told you about this, but it gives you an idea about how fucked up my life has been. I fell for a nigga on the down low, Trina. If I shared with you all of the things that I allowed him to do to me, or all of the things that I'd done to him, you'd throw up."

This was bad. Real bad. I couldn't believe that Bryson was on the DL. He had so many women in his circle, beautiful women, too. I'd seen him with chicks who looked as if they were Hollywood made. They loved Bryson's dirty underwear and would do anything to be with him. I was outdone by this news. I figured Keith didn't have a clue about his brother. He and Bryson were very close, but I was almost positive that something like this wouldn't sit right with Keith.

Evelyn interrupted my thoughts. "I don't need any more trouble, Trina, so again, keep this between us. I get that you've been mad at me and you may not care what Bryson will do to me, if this gets out. But, please, have some concern for my well-being."

This time, I stood and paced the floor. Evelyn had put me on the spot. Maybe I needed to speak to Bryson first, before I decided what to do with this information. There was still a chance that Evelyn was being untruthful.

"Girl, if you're lying about this, shame on you. You need to seek help and—"

Evelyn pounded her leg with her fist. "I'm not lying! The truth is, I do believe that I need to talk to a professional who may be able to help me deal with all of this pain. I've been dealing with it for a long time, and I've never sought help from when I experienced my father beating me and my mother, him making us homeless or for having sex with me. I should have gotten help years ago, but I never did. Maybe all of this craziness wouldn't be happening, and maybe I could've figured out how to be a better friend."

Evelyn's words made me reflect to when she used to come to school with black eyes and with bruises on her arms and legs, compliments of her father. Kayla and I felt so bad for her. My mother even pitched in to help when Evelyn's father threw her and her mother out of the house. They stayed with us for a few months then went to live in a shelter. The people at the shelter found them a place to live, but it wasn't long before her mother let her dad back in. The abuse continued and the rest was history. I guess that a part of me couldn't blame Evelyn for being so screwed up. She wasn't lying when she said she needed some help.

"I applaud you for wanting to get some counseling, and it's not exactly a bad thing. I've had my issues too, and I just realized what was holding me back when it came to Keith. I talked to him about it, and I feel much better."

"That's the thing. You have somebody to talk to. I don't. I keep all of this stuff bottled up inside of me, and I haven't said much to you or Kayla about my issues because I don't want to be judged. Just know that I'm sorry for everything. No matter if you decide to forgive me or not, I'm sorry and please tell Keith I'm sorry too."

Right at that moment, the front door opened. Keith walked in with a smile, but it vanished when he saw Evelyn sitting on the couch.

"What is she doing here?" he asked with a frown on his face.

I didn't like his tone, but I understood where it was coming from. "She came over to apologize to us about what happened."

"Apologize? I don't need an apology and neither do you. What I need is for Evelyn to get off my couch and leave. Right now."

Evelyn blinked tears from her eyes and stood up. No words could express how bad I felt. She was so unstable. I didn't want her to leave here, feeling as if everyone was against her. I tried to settle this with Keith, but he wasn't trying to hear it.

"Keith, calm down. Let me finish talking to her, and then we'll—"

"I am calm, and I will remain calm, as long as she exits." He walked to the door and opened it. "Peace."

Evelyn blinked away her tears and her breath staggered. She was fighting back all that was inside of her. I wanted to tell her not to leave, but I didn't want to argue with Keith. Instead, I walked behind her and tapped her shoulder. She turned around.

"Give me a hug before you go. Stay strong and we'll talk soon enough."

She threw her arms around me and held me tight. So tight, as if she didn't want to let go. When she did, she barely looked at Keith who stood at the door with a mean mug. After giving him one last look, she left. I slowly closed the door and turned to him.

"I know what you're going to say, but she's going through a lot right now. I tried not to sympathize with her, but you know how I am."

Keith gave me a dirty look then walked away. He went into the kitchen and I followed. He opened the fridge, pulled out a beer, and popped the cap. The strange gaze in his eyes was still there.

"What is it?" I said. "Why do you keep looking at me like that?"

Keith guzzled down the beer and then wiped across his mouth. "I almost hate to ask you this, but something here ain't right. Were you and Evelyn ever lovers, or should I say, are the two of you still lovers?"

If there ever was a time when I wanted to smack the shit out of Keith, this was it. How dare he ask me such a question? What a gotdamn insult.

"You can't be serious," I snapped.

"I'm very serious. Because I don't understand how you could've let her back into this house. After all that she's done, her lies and games, you felt a need to open the door and let her in here? I don't give a rat's ass what she's been through. Hell, we all go through things, but we don't go around manipulating people, trying to screw people's significant others and telling lies about them, do we?"

"She's a little off, Keith. I suggested that she gets some help. Hopefully, she'll take my advice."

He slammed the bottle of beer on the table. "A little off? No, she is way off and wacky as hell. I don't ever want her in this house again."

"Yeah, well, you're way off too by suggesting that she and I are lovers. I guess you're a wacko too. And in case you forgot, I live here too. I don't tell you who is or isn't allowed in here, and it's wrong for you to try to tell me."

"What I say goes. She's not welcome here, Trina. If you don't like it, you know what you can do."

Keith walked past me and left the kitchen. The last thing I wanted was to get into another heated argument with him, so I decided to let him cool off and rethink his position. He went upstairs, and I grabbed my purse and keys from the couch. I looked like a bum in my jeans and half shirt, but I needed to get out of there. I also needed to go talk to Bryson. If what Evelyn said was true, Keith needed to know. I wasn't about to keep any more secrets from him.

Taking my chances, I went to a worksite where Keith and I had taken Bryson some lunch earlier in the week. It was a big project that he was working on, so I prayed that he was there so we could talk.

I arrived at the location, seeing several construction workers with hard hats on. It was rather noisy, and I started to think that maybe this was a bad idea. My thoughts were quickly washed away when I saw Bryson and another man standing real close to each other. They appeared to be indulged in a deep conversation, and I knew flirting eyes when I saw them. There was too much smiling going on and a bunch of lip licking, too. I parked my car, and as I moved toward them, I saw Bryson back away from the man. The second his eyes shifted in my direction, the man turned around to see who I was. Bryson said something to him, and he walked away.

"What's up, sis-in-law," he said with a smile. "You know better than to come out here without any lunch in your hand, and where is my brother at?"

"He's at home, mad as hell at me."

"What for?"

"I'll tell you in a minute. That's why I'm here. Is there anywhere private where we can talk?"

Bryson nodded and told me to follow him into a construction trailer that was piled with junk, including a desk, several folding chairs, and orange street cones. He invited me to have a seat in one of the chairs.

"Can I get you a bottled water or soda?"

"No, I'm fine."

Bryson got a bottled water from the fridge then took a seat behind the wooden desk.

"What's on your mind? Keith's been causing you some headaches?"

"No, not exactly, but one of my friends have been. That would be Evelyn. She came to see me today, and she said some disturbing things to me about you."

Bryson almost dropped the bottled water that was close to his lips. It splashed on his shirt and he wiped it. "What did she say that was so disturbing? I could say some disturbing things about her too, but I'm skeptical about going there because she's your friend."

"I'll get straight to the point. She said that you were on the DL. Claimed she caught you having sex with a tranny and showed me the balance of some money you put into her account to keep quiet. I totally do not believe her, but I needed to hear what was up from your mouth. Why would she say something like that about you, if it wasn't true?"

Bryson leaned back in the chair and scratched his head. "Because she's fucking crazy, that's why. I swear I be messing around with some weird-ass chicks. But this here takes the cake. I've never heard no shit like this before, and where do these women be getting their stories from? Books?"

I laughed because he had a point. "It's funny that you say that because I recently read a book by Nikki Michelle, *Bi-Satisfied*. It was along the same lines as what Evelyn claimed she saw you indulged in, so maybe she read the same book."

Bryson laughed. "Maybe so. But, uh, just so you know, I don't get down like that. Not me; never."

Bryson guzzled down the water, while tapping his fingers on the desk. As we talked, he tapped faster. His leg shook and he had the same shocking look in his eyes that I'd had when Kayla confronted me about what Cedric suspected about me.

When the direction of my eyes traveled to Bryson's fingers, he stopped tapping them and squeezed his hand.

I let him know what was on my mind. "Let me just say this to you, okay, Bryson? I don't know if Keith ever mentioned this to you before, but I used to be bisexual. My family disowned me, and until this day, they still do. I had a very difficult time telling anyone what was going on with me, and I kept that secret away from my friends for a very long time. You may already know that the chick who stabbed Keith was my lover. I have to live with that, and it still pains me to know that my lies could have killed him. I don't care what your sexual preferences are. You know that Keith and I will love you regardless. But do me a favor and please tell him the truth, if indeed you are having sex with men. I say that because hearing this from other people will be damaging.

If Evelyn has any proof, or if what she's saying is factual, it's just a matter of time when your secret will no longer be a secret. All the money in the world will not keep her mouth closed."

Bryson looked away, swallowed, and then looked at me with a devious gaze. "Didn't you hear what I said? I told you that bitch was lying, and I'm not about to confess to something that ain't true. Keith told me about your little girlfriend, but if that's how you chose to get down, then don't come in here trying to push that shit off on me. I got a gang of women who can vouch for me. They know what I stand for. It's called pussy. That's what my heart desires, and unfortunately, your friend is only upset because hers wasn't good enough for me. Now, I have to get back to work. But before I do, you may want to tell your friend that if any of her lies leak elsewhere, well, I can show her better than I can tell her."

Seeing that Bryson was getting pretty upset with me, I stood to go. "If she is lying, then I guess you have nothing to worry about. If you are, then you're the one who has to deal with the repercussions. Thanks for listening to me, and you have my word that I will not bring any of this up to Keith."

"I hope not. And please keep that bullshit to yourself."

On that note, I left. I knew for a fact that Evelyn wasn't lying. Bryson was. But at this point, there was nothing that I could do but keep quiet until the shit hit the fan.

Chapter 16

Kayla

Evelyn told Trina what had happened and Trina told me. I wanted to laugh at what Cedric did, but to me, it really wasn't a laughing matter. Don't get me wrong. I despised Evelyn to the fullest. I would never be a friend to her again, but Cedric was out of line.

With that being said, I was going to contact him and say something, but I decided against it. I said that Jacoby was my priority and that he was. I'd been making sure that he handled his business at school, I limited his time with Adrianne a little bit, and the two of us spent a lot of quality time together talking, hanging out, and enjoying each other's company. I made it clear to him that I had his back and he now knew it, more than ever.

Jacoby and I had just gotten back from Froyo, getting some frozen yogurt. The second we got out of the car, Cedric was parking. He hadn't been over to see our new place, but I'd given him the address and told him all about it. He was in the process of looking for a place too. A few days ago, he mentioned that someone was interested in buying the house. I guess he'd stopped by to tell me all about it and to check out the new place we called home.

"Damn, that's how I get played?" he said, looking at our yogurt with his hands held out. "Where's mine at?"

"Jacoby bought this for me," I said. "Since I didn't have any money."

Jacoby said, "What's up," to Cedric and walked ahead of us. Since I'd known about the incident, he kind of shied away from Cedric. I told him to stop doing that because Cedric would pick up on it and say something, as he'd done before.

"No money," Cedric shouted. "Woman, please. If your money is gone, you need that ass kicked."

Jacoby had already opened the door to our apartment, so we followed and went inside. Cedric looked up at the vaulted ceiling in the foyer and checked out the spacious living room area with double bay windows.

"What kind of apartment is this?" he said. "How did you find this place?"

"By driving around. It's nice, isn't it? Let me show you the kitchen."

"I prefer to see the bedroom," he joked. I rolled my eyes at him. "Not to do anything with you, but just in case I may want to move in another unit around here."

"Please, no way. I don't want to be close to you, and I think it's best that you move waaaay on the other side of town."

Jacoby was already sitting at the kitchen table when we entered. He was eating his yogurt while watching TV. Cedric spoke about how fabulous the kitchen was, and then he sat at the table with Jacoby.

"What's up with you, man? Why have you been ignoring me?" Cedric asked.

Jacoby shrugged, looked at Cedric then looked at the TV again. "I'm not ignoring you. I was just looking at TV, trying to see if the game was on."

"That's cool, but, uh, how about we get together for the weekend. Go to one of the basketball games in Miami and see who's really bringing the Heat. A friend of mine got a yacht down there, too. He has a son around your age and we can hang out with them on the high seas and have a good time."

Jacoby nodded while rubbing his forehead. "Maybe so. I'll let you know for sure by tomorrow. Adrianne and I had plans, but I'll see if I can cancel."

"Adrianne can wait. Besides, she sees you more than I do. You need some space and time to just go do you, if you know what I mean."

"Like I said, we'll see."

I didn't want to interfere, but I could see how uncomfortable Jacoby was. "Jacoby, why don't you go call Trey back? He called earlier, saying that he needed some assistance with his homework. Go call him before it gets too late, and you get all wrapped up in that game."

Jacoby got up from the table and walked away. Cedric grabbed his arm, causing Jacoby to jump as if he were startled. All Cedric did was hold out his hand for dap.

"I can't get no holla later or hand slap before you head to your room? I'm not staying long, but don't forget to call me tomorrow."

"I won't," Jacoby said then slapped his hand against Cedric's. Jacoby also gave him a hug, too, and then he left the room.

"I'm telling you that something is up with our son," Cedric said. "I don't like it either, and I think he may need counseling. I also think that seeing me lying there almost dead has affected him in a major way. Every time I mention that day to him, he gets real uptight."

"I think you're making too much of this, Cedric. Jacoby has a lot on his mind with school and his girlfriend. Going away to Miami this weekend may be a good thing for him, but please be careful with my only child."

"Sure, Miss Too Overprotective. I wouldn't want him to fall off the yacht by accident and go missing in the water. You'd probably kill me."

My face fell flat after that comment. Cedric shot me a peculiar look and stared at me. Why would he make a comment like that? Did he know something that he wasn't saying? More than that, was his tail planning to kill my son? That comment rubbed me the wrong way.

I snapped my finger. "You know what? I just thought about something. I'm supposed to go take Jacoby for his SAT prep test this weekend. He's on the schedule to take it, and I don't want him to miss it. You may have to plan that trip to Miami on another date."

"All right. I'll check my calendar and see what's up."

Cedric's cell phone rang. He looked to see who it was. He excused himself and went outside on the balcony to take the call. I had moved to the other side of the kitchen, and I kept seeing him peeking around the corner to see where I'd gone to. I moved closer to the sliding doors, trying to make out what he was saying. All I heard was a lot of whispers. Whispers that made me nervous.

So nervous that when he came back inside, I questioned him.

"Why were you out there whispering?" I asked while standing by the island.

"I wasn't whispering. And if I was, that's because who I speak to ain't your business."

"If it's not my business then it must have been Evelyn. Then again, it couldn't have been her because I heard you beat her like she stole something from you. I didn't know you'd gotten so violent."

Cedric shot me that peculiar look again then walked over to stand in front of me. He eased his hands in his pockets and jiggled his keys. "Yeah, well, when you keep on getting fucked over by no-good women who want your money one minute, then want to kill you the next minute, you kind of get tired of the shit. At some point, the only way you can deal with them is by being violent, because it's the only language they understand. The bottom line is, Evelyn got what she deserved. And everybody else who wishes to fuck me over will get the same thing too. With that, I'm out. I can't check out the rest of the place, because I have somewhere I need to be. Don't forget to tell Jacoby to call me, either way."

I nodded and watched as Cedric strutted toward the door.

"By the way, what about the house?" I yelled after him. "Any buyers?"

He turned at the door. "We'll talk about that the next time I stop by. Gotta go, but before I do, I wanted to let you know that I fired Cynthia."

"Why?" I said with a frown. "She was very nice."

"Nice, but too gotdamn nosy."

Cedric walked out. I hated to hear that about Cynthia, but was it possible that Cedric had already put two and two together? He was a very smart man, and the least I could do was try my best to stay on his good side, just in case his suspicions grew.

I was so worried about how much Cedric knew that I decided to follow him and go see what he was up to. I also thought it would be wise for me to stop by his house and do some snooping around. I had to be sure that he wasn't plotting against me and Jacoby. For some reason, he'd been extremely nice, which was kind of odd for Cedric. Yeah, he'd been near death before. That was definitely a reason to make someone have a change of heart. But what he'd done to Evelyn proved to me that Cedric wasn't the changed man he was claiming to be.

I rushed to Jacoby's room to tell him I'd be right back. He didn't bother to ask where I was going because he was on the phone. I hurried into my car, suspecting that Cedric would be heading toward the highway. Sure enough, he was. He had just made a left turn, and I had to go through a red light to prevent him from getting away from me. There were several cars between us, and I could barely keep up because Cedric was driving fast. I could see that he was on his cell phone. He didn't end the call until he got off at the Forest Park exit. That was where he exited his car and walked up to a white man who appeared to be waiting for him. They shook hands then sat on a bench, talking for a while. The man passed Cedric an envelope, but they kept on talking. There was no way for me to see what was inside of the envelope because I was too far away. As I moved closer and squinted, Cedric tucked the envelope into his jacket. He exchanged another handshake with the man then left.

After that, I followed him to a restaurant on Manchester. That was where he met a woman outside. She appeared to be a classy woman who kind of reminded me of myself. She was very tall and could have easily been a model. Truthfully, she almost looked like me, but I was healthier than she was. I watched as she and Cedric sat in his car and kissed. It was pretty intense, and then they exited the car. Cedric held her waist and patted her ass as they went inside. Less than a minute later, they came back out and headed to his car. With so many people waiting outside to be served, I guessed that the wait time was too long for them. Her back was against Cedric's car and he stood in front of her. I saw his hands creep up her dress, but she playfully smacked it. The way they acted toward each other, I could instantly tell that this wasn't a new relationship. Yet again, they shared a lengthy kiss then got into separate cars. Cedric followed her, and I followed him. I thought they were going to his place, but instead, they stopped at her place, which was less than a mile away from where he lived. It was obvious what they were getting ready to get into, since Cedric tossed his jacket over his shoulder and followed her into her house, while wiggling his tie away from his neck. After seeing that, I sped off. I was feeling some kind of way about my ex-husband being with this woman. Yes, a tiny part of me was jealous, but a huge part of me was delighted about the decision I'd made to proceed with the divorce. For him to bring up sex, when in my presence, was wrong on so many different levels. He knew better. I wouldn't dare go there with him again.

Cedric was going to be busy for a long time, so I drove to his house. I still had a key to let myself in, but I was nervous about going inside and snooping. The second I pushed the door open, my cell phone rang, causing me to jump. It was Trina. I hurried to answer, just so she wouldn't call back and rattle my nerves again.

"Hello," I whispered.

"Why are you whispering?"

I raised my voice up a notch. Didn't make sense to whisper anyway, especially since no one was there. "No reason," I said. "What's up?"

"Nothing much. I wanted to holler for a minute, about Evelyn."

Evelyn. Evelyn. Evelyn. I didn't have time to discuss Evelyn right now.

"Listen, Trina, I'm kind of busy. And to be honest, I'm getting kind of tired of hearing about Evelyn and her drama. I'm not trying to be rude, but can you please find someone else to talk about?"

Trina hesitated with her response. "Don't worry about it. I'll talk to you later."

Trina hung up on me. I surely didn't care. I mean, enough already with Evelyn and her mess. I seriously couldn't understand why Trina was still trying to hold on to their friendship. I was going to tell Trina how I really felt about this. But for now, I had a bigger fish to fry.

I dropped my cell phone into my purse. The first place I went to was where Cedric spent most of his time. That was in his office. The next thing I did was search through his computer. I examined his files and looked at the last links in his browser that he'd visited. I read some of his recent letters and scanned through his calendar to see if anything was out of the ordinary. Most of the things that I saw were related to business. I didn't find much on his computer, so I began to check his drawers. Yet again, much of what I found was business related, but I did find a porn magazine, condoms, and several pictures. I flipped through pictures of the woman he was currently with. They were naked pictures, and I found myself a little jealous because she had it going on. I also saw several "get well soon" cards from her. Touching messages were written inside and she stressed how much she loved him. Like I'd said, it was obvious that their relationship had been going on for quite some time. Joy made that quite clear in her letters and cards.

I came up empty with my drawer search, so I lifted the pillows on the couch and searched underneath them. I checked the bookshelves, and that was where I found a 9 mm that made me more nervous. I didn't dare touch it, but I walked away from the bookshelves and looked underneath a huge rug that covered the hardwood floors. Nothing. Nothing at all, so I left Cedric's office and went to his bedroom. Didn't have much luck there, but I found several more letters from Joy who was more than excited about our divorce. According to her, she couldn't wait for Cedric to sell the house, so the two of them could move in together. That way, she could take care of him, since I failed to do so. I wanted to go to her house and slap her, like I'd slapped Evelyn for being so stupid. Women sure didn't know how to stick together, and they would quickly throw you under the bus, when it came to a man. One day, I'd give her a piece of my mind and tell her what I really thought of the comments about me in her letters. She was on the outside looking in and didn't have a clue what it was like to be married to Cedric.

With an attitude, I continued my search. Went to the basement then found myself back in Cedric's office. I stood in the doorway looking around. My eyes shifted to a mail tray on one of the shelves that I'd overlooked. Inside of the tray were envelopes that contained bills. But there were also four envelopes wrapped with a rubber band. The envelopes hadn't been opened, but there were letters inside. The letters came from the correctional facility where Paula Daniels was at. They were all addressed to him. Eager to see what she had written to him, I panicked as I tore open one of the letters. It was short, and according to her, she needed to speak to him about something important. She didn't say what it was until I read the next letter. That was when she got specific and wrote that it was imperative that she spoke to him about something with Jacoby. She stressed how sorry she was, apologized for trying to kill him, but said she felt as if he needed to know the truth.

I hurried to stuff the letters into my purse. Looked around for more of them, but didn't find any. Searched for a few minutes more then gave up. I left, feeling as if this situation would, eventually, turn ugly. Maybe Jacoby and I needed to get ahead of this and talk to Cedric? Seemed like Paula was eager to bust Jacoby out, and it was best that Cedric heard it from us, instead of her. I remained in the car in deep thought about what to do. And when my cell phone rang, I grabbed it from my purse and put the phone up to my ear.

"Hello," I said.

"I have a question for you," Cedric said in a serious tone.

My stomach twisted in a knot. I could feel a sheen of sweat forming on my forehead.

"Wha . . . what is it?"

"Why are you in my house?"

This time, my stomach hit the floor. I had no answer; my mouth was stuck.

"I have cameras in there," he said. "Didn't want what happened to me before to happen again. I've seen you going through my things. And the only other question I have for you is why are those letters from Paula any concern of yours?"

I was cold busted. Couldn't think of a lie fast enough to get me out of this. I wasn't sure if my made-up explanation would suffice or not, but I went for it anyway.

"The truth is, I still love you, Cedric. A part of me regrets signing those divorce papers, and I could kick myself for doing so. I suspected that you were on the phone earlier with another woman and I was jealous. After you left my house, I attempted to follow you, but I lost you somewhere on the highway. I thought you would meet the woman here, so I came by to see what was up. You know how nosy I am, so I started looking around to see what I could find. Your relationship with Joy hurts me, and I didn't appreciate the letters I found from Paula. I hate her for what she tried to do to you, so I took the letters to dispose of them. You haven't been keeping in touch with her, have you? I truly hope not, Cedric, especially after what she did to you."

There was a crisp silence over the phone. I hoped that Cedric believed me, but maybe I rambled on too long. I waited with bated breath to hear his response.

He cleared his throat. "Hell, no, I haven't been keeping in touch with her. I couldn't care less about what she has to say, and I have no intentions to read those dumb letters. If she continues to write them, I'm going to turn them over to the police. I already have some people involved who will make those letters stop. As for Joy, she's a nice woman. I don't want you having any regrets about our divorce, only because I do believe you made the right decision for both of us. So don't sweat it, baby. You know damn well that you can have a piece of me whenever you want it. All you have to do is say the word."

Cedric laughed. So did I, feeling a bit relieved. Just a little, because I was still hoping like hell that the letters stopped.

Chapter 17

Trina

Keith's big dick was so far up in me that I couldn't even think straight. I couldn't move and I was on the verge of a shaky orgasm. Make-up sex between us was always the best. This time around, I apologized for the incident with Evelyn. I made Keith feel as if I were on his side, but the truth was, I was caught in the middle.

I'd spoken to Evelyn and expressed how sorry I was about Keith's ill treatment. I tried to explain his position, and Evelyn insisted she understood. What I didn't tell her, though, was that I'd gone to see Bryson. I didn't find it necessary to tell her my thoughts about what I discovered during our conversation. That would only give her more ammunition, and I didn't want to stir her up.

What I wanted was more of Keith. He was now down below, sucking my well dry. My thighs were locked on his face and my eyes were squeezed tight. I could barely catch my breath, and I pounded his back, letting him know how spectacular his tongue tricks felt.

"Baby, you are the motherfucking man! My man, so keep doing that shit, only how you can do it!"

I loved to stroke his ego. Seeing him smile always made me feel good. His tongue snaked in and out of my folds. He tickled my pearl then turned me over to tackle my goodness from behind. I kicked, screamed and begged for him to keep at, so I'd come again. Within minutes, my request was honored. I was spent; he was too. He crawled next to me in bed and lay flat on his back while taking deep breaths. While staring at the ceiling, he rubbed his chest.

"Did I tell you how much I love you today?" he said.

I turned sideways and rubbed my hand on his chest. "No, you didn't tell me, but you sure did show me."

Keith massaged my ass when I laid my leg across his. "I did, didn't I? But I'm gon' need for you to calm your hot self down. Just so you know, you are wearing my ass out."

"Good. And when I get finished with this shower, I'm going to wear you out some more. So get ready."

I got out of bed and headed for the bathroom to take a shower. I thought Keith was going to join me, but he didn't. With him not being in the shower with me, I took my time and indulged in a lengthy one. I shaved my legs and trimmed my toenails. It took me about an hour to get finished, and after I was done, I opened the door and could hear Keith downstairs talking. Better yet, yelling at somebody. I was so sure that Evelyn had shown back up, but as I jetted down the stairs, I saw Keith standing in the living room with Bryson. Their argument was pretty intense. I'd never seen them go at it like this before. They stood face to face with each other, talking shit.

"I'll say it again," Keith hissed. "Watch your mouth or I will drop your punk ass on the floor."

Bryson folded his arms across his buffed chest and a smirk appeared on his face. "Do what you must, little brother. The floor is all yours."

I quickly ran over and squeezed my short self in between them. "Whatever is going on here, it doesn't need to be settled with a fistfight. I know the two of you can do better than this, so calm down and chill."

Keith ignored me and inched forward, squeezing me more. "It can be settled when he gives our mother her money back. If not, I will handle you myself."

Bryson stepped forward and I eased out of the way. "I will give the money back when I choose to. This really ain't your damn business, and I'm getting tired of your threats."

"Maybe so. But here's a promise."

Keith reached out and slammed his fist right at Bryson's jaw. The blow sent him staggering backward, and he tripped over the table behind him and fell hard.

"How was that for a promise?" Keith said. "If you don't give the money back, another one of those punches will be coming your way."

Bryson tightened his fist and charged toward Keith like a raging mad bull. He wound up slamming Keith on the floor and they went at it tough. So tough that I had to scramble out of the way.

"Stop it," I yelled to get their attention. "Or else I'll call the police!"

My police threat fell on deaf ears and frightened no one. They kept at it and were pounding the hell out of each other. Keith was getting the best of Bryson, but then all of a sudden, the tables turned. He punched Keith in his mouth and I witnessed my man's blood splatter. I rushed in and started hitting Bryson on the back of his head to distract him so Keith could get the upper hand again. My interference distracted Bryson, but it didn't halt his punches. The next one he delivered landed right at my face, particularly at my right eye that throbbed and felt as if it had been knocked from the socket. I backed away and held my face. Keith lost it. But as he charged at Bryson, he sent Keith backing up with a hard blow to his stomach that dropped him to one knee.

"Now what, motherfucker?" Spit flew from Bryson's mouth and his chest heaved in and out. He pounded it hard then looked at me. "You dyke-ass bitch, stay the hell out of family affairs."

I was stunned by Bryson's actions, and I couldn't hold back all that was inside of me. My man was hurt and so was I.

"Screw you, you grimy, down-low-ass nigga. How in the hell you gon' call me a dyke, and yo' ass out there fucking men? Or should I say, allowing them to fuck you?"

The direction of Bryson's eyes shot over to Keith. His eyes, however, were locked on me. I could tell he was waiting for me to say more, but I fell back on the couch and held my eye.

Keith took deep breaths then addressed Bryson. "Get the hell out of here. Now! And don't you ever come back!"

Bryson stood for a moment, looking as if he wanted to say something or as if he wanted to apologize. Instead, he rushed off and swung the door open. He left, leaving it wide open.

Keith limped over to me while holding his side. "Why did you say that to him?" he asked. "Do you know something that I don't?"

I was about to tell him that my words had slipped, and I said them to upset Bryson. But then I decided against it. "I don't know if it's true or not, but Evelyn said—"

"To hell with what Evelyn said," Keith shouted. He shouted so loudly that my whole body shook.

"You're right," I hurried to say. "But please go talk to your brother. He has all the answers you're looking for."

Sweat was on the thick wrinkles that lined Keith's forehead. The mean mug was locked there, even when he rubbed my face and bent over to kiss my swollen eye. "Put some ice on that. I'm leaving to go find Bryson. I'll be back later."

Before I could say anything, he jetted.

I was so worried about Keith being gone. Hours had passed, and I kept calling his cell phone, but he wouldn't answer. My eye was bloodshot red, and by tomorrow it would be worse. I lay across the bed, wondering where my man was and if he was okay. I now regretted what I'd said to Bryson. Keith seemed very concerned about it, and that was the only thing that probably caused him to leave. If something happened to him again, because of me, I would never forgive myself.

I wasn't sure what time it was, but when I woke up, Keith sat on the bed next to me. He touched my face and apologized for what Bryson had done.

"You don't have to apologize," I said, slowly sitting up. "It wasn't your fault." I looked at the gloom expression on his face, knowing that he had caught up with Bryson. "So, how did it go? Did you talk to him?"

Keith nodded. "I did."

"And?"

"And I don't know what to believe. He told me about your visit. I was surprised to hear that you went to go see him, without saying anything to me."

"I wanted to, but I didn't want to confront you with something that may not have been true."

"Regardless, you should have said something to me. In not doing so, it makes me feel as if I can't trust you. I don't like secrets, Trina. I thought you learned your lesson about keeping them."

"I have, but this situation was different. With Evelyn being the source who provided the information, I wasn't sure how to handle things. That's why I went to go see Bryson, so that he could defend what she'd said."

Keith fell back on the bed and lay flat on his back. He put his hands behind his head and gazed at the spinning ceiling fan. "After speaking to him," he said, "what's your take on the matter? What conclusion did you come to?"

I lay silent for a while then slightly shrugged. I didn't want to say what I thought for real. I could tell Keith was hurt; I didn't want to hurt him anymore.

"The truth, Trina. I want the truth."

"Based on how I was when I tried to hide my preference from everyone, I have to be honest and say that I believe Bryson is on the down low. I'm not a hundred percent sure, but Evelyn was paid a substantial amount of money to keep her mouth shut. If you mother is missing some money, maybe that's the money Bryson gave to Evelyn."

"He has a gambling problem, and he's always taking money from the family stash. Just not that much. Either way, you didn't believe him when he told you he wasn't involved with men?"

"No. Unfortunately, I didn't."

Keith lay silent for a minute, and then he got off the bed. He opened the bathroom door then turned to face me. "Just so you know, I didn't believe him either."

Keith shut the door behind him, after he went into the bathroom. I shook my head, upset that there seemed to be no end to the drama.

Chapter 18

Evelyn

I was sitting on the couch, eating buttery popcorn and watching *Scandal*. I was so into it that I barely heard the knocks on my door. Whoever it was they were going to stay out there because, number one, the person didn't buzz me, and number two, *Scandal* was too good to be interrupted. I ignored the knocks then heard Bryson's voice, loud and clear.

"Open the door! You and I got ourselves a little problem!"

I rolled my eyes and continued to chomp on my popcorn. "Go away, Bryson! I'm busy."

I got back to watching *Scandal,* and minutes later, I heard a loud thud. The second thud was louder, and the third one caused the whole door to break off the hinges and come crashing down. I jumped and sent the bowl of popcorn flying at Bryson, when he rushed in. He resembled a madman in a horror movie. Sweat ran down his face, his teeth ground and his shirt was ripped. There was also a long scar on the side of his face. I quickly moved out of the way and jumped on top of the couch. I lifted my foot to keep him away from me and threatened to kick.

"Bitch, didn't I tell you to keep your mother-fucking mouth shut!"

I played clueless. "I didn't say a word to anyone. What are you talking about?"

My eyes shifted toward the doorway. If I could just make it to the door and run to the elevator, security would see me. Then someone would be able to help me. But if I couldn't make it to the doorway, there would be no way out of this.

I took my chances and jumped over the couch. I sprinted toward the door, but this was one time I hated my hair was long. Bryson grabbed my hair from behind, yanking it so hard that I fell backward. He straddled the top of me, and all I remembered seeing was him raising his fist and slamming it into my face. After that, I saw darkness, but felt numerous blows being delivered to my body. Blows that made my insides burn and hurt—hurt so bad that I seriously wanted to die.

I didn't know what day it was, how many hours had gone by or where I was at. For a while, I thought I was dead because of the numerous white lights that flashed before me. The last things I could picture in my mind were Bryson's angry face and his powerful fists. That was all, until somebody shook my shoulder and kept calling my name. I cracked my eyes open and everything in front of me was a blur. I could hear a voice, and the person in front of me looked to be a doctor.

"Next of kin," he said. "Any family members? If so, who would you like for me to reach out to?"

The doctor showed me a piece of paper and pen. He placed it on the table in front of me and I began to write. The person's name and number I wrote was Trina's. Underneath her name, I scribbled the word, sister. After that, my eyes shut again.

I woke up, hearing a bunch of chatter. My vision was still blurred when I opened my eyes. I could barely focus. I blinked and saw Trina standing next to me. She squeezed my hand with hers and kept calling my name. I wasn't sure if I was dreaming. Trina wasn't smiling and a deeply concerned look was on her face. She called my name again. This time, I nodded to let her know that I'd heard her.

"Can you hear me?"

I nodded again and spilled a soft, "Yes."

She released a deep breath. "Thank God. Thank you, Jesus." Apparently, she'd been praying for me. I opened my mouth to speak again, but it hurt so badly because of the tube in my mouth. With that, I stayed silent.

"Don't worry," Trina said. "You're going to be fine."

A slow tear dripped from the corner of my eye. My whole body was hurting. I tried to move around, but couldn't. Tried to move my arms, couldn't do that either. Attempted to move my toes, but no luck. I closed my eyes and had flashbacks of Bryson beating the shit out of me. This time, I didn't have to exaggerate like I did when Cedric attacked me. This was real. Everything that I played out in my head was real. Bryson tried to kill me. I wondered, who stopped him? Thought about if he was in jail. Hopefully he was, but I seriously didn't know.

What I did know was that he'd found out what I'd told Trina, only, about his down-low status. I had only shared that information with her. I begged her not to say anything. I knew that if she did, it would come to this. It was evident that she didn't care. It probably pleased her heart to see me laid up like this. She and Kayla always wanted to see me at my lowest point. Well, this was it. I hoped she was happy, even though she didn't look as if she was.

I opened my eyes and stared at Trina. This time, she displayed a forced grin. For some reason, I could feel her squeezing my hand again, but I couldn't feel much else but a severe headache. It was difficult for me to speak, but I had to ask her a question. I needed to know something, and I wanted to make her feel horrible for betraying me.

I stretched my mouth and mumbled to her. "Why?"

Trina inched closer so she could hear me. "Why what? What did you say?"

"Why did you tell Bryson what I'd told you? I begged you not to . . . to say anything. You promised me that you wouldn't. Why, Trina? Did you want him to kill me?"

A fast tear fell down Trina's face. She couldn't even respond. After a few minutes, she whispered that she was sorry.

Yeah, I was sorry too. Sorry that, eventually, she'd have to pay for running her big mouth.

Chapter 19

Kayla

I was in awe as Trina sat at my kitchen table, asking me to go to the hospital with her to see Evelyn. Trina claimed that it would brighten Evelyn's day and give her hope. Seeing me would be the best thing ever, and it would give us a chance to mend our friendship. There was no doubt that I felt terrible for Evelyn. I truly wished her well, but going to the hospital to see her was something that I didn't want to do. Trina acted as if she didn't understand why I didn't want to go. So, I had to remind her why I was standing my ground about not going.

"I'm sorry, but I'm having a difficult time forgiving a woman—no, let me correct myself—my best friend who slept with my husband, got pregnant by him, used his money, lied to me about it, stabbed me in my back, preferred that I be homeless, and told my son that I'd lied to him about who his father was. I could go on and on, Trina, but I won't. If you've forgiven her, that's on you. More power to you."

Trina massaged her forehead. "I know she's done some horrible things, but I feel so guilty about telling Bryson what she'd told me. If I'd kept my mouth shut, none of this would've happened. I'm stuck in the middle, trying to be there for her, and trying to be there for Keith who has taken Bryson's side. His defense is that Evelyn had a gun and threatened to kill him. Claimed all he did was go to her place to talk, but she pulled a gun on him. According to him, he was forced to defend himself because she was acting like a maniac."

"Well, you did say there were bullet holes in the walls, right? And how do you know that what he said happened isn't the truth?"

"Because I witnessed how upset Bryson was about being outed. And remember, I was on the receiving end of one of his rages too. He's still denying everything, and I don't believe anything he says. Keith and I keep clashing about this, too. I guess the truth will come out, during the trial."

"Maybe it will, but if I were you, I wouldn't put my money on Evelyn."

I got up and went to the fridge to get a soda. A part of me was livid with Trina for being so foolish. But I didn't want to say anything to hurt her feelings more. She felt responsible for this and had been running to the hospital almost every day to check on Evelyn. Trina said she was getting better, but Bryson had broken her ribs and given her a concussion. She could barely walk and needed therapy. Her headaches were severe, and Trina stressed how much pain she'd been in.

"I understand all of that, Kayla, but everything you just mentioned is in the past. You're not going to harp on that forever, are you? The last time I checked, Cedric was the one who caused you the most damage. If you can forgive him, surely you can forgive Evelyn. I think you should go see her."

I couldn't hold back any longer. "Trina, personally, I don't care what you or Evelyn thinks. I forgave Cedric because he was my husband. He took responsibility for his actions. In addition to that, he didn't leave me high and dry. So please don't compare Evelyn to Cedric. There is a big difference."

Trina pushed and cocked her head back to look at me. "So, let me get this straight. The only reason you forgave Cedric was because he put millions into your bank account? Damn, Kayla, how selfish can you be? How can you make this all about money, when your friend was in the hospital clinging on for dear life? Excuse me for thinking you were better than that."

The guilt trip was in full effect. And, no, Trina didn't just go there, did she? I slammed my soda on the island and walked up to her, darting my finger. "How dare you call me selfish because I refuse to break my neck and run out of here for a tramp who brought this mess on herself? You have no darn idea what I've been through. When I was down and out, nobody was there for me. Surely not Evelyn who put me out of her place, knowing that I had nowhere to go. So while you think I should run to her bedside, I don't get it. Please help me understand this, because I am deeply confused."

Trina didn't appreciate my tone or aggressiveness, as I'd moved closer to make my case. She picked up her purse and put the straps on her shoulder. This time, she was much calmer than I was.

"I can't say anything to help you understand. But what I will do is ask you to reflect on the bond the three of us used to have. We were like sisters, and a long time ago, we never allowed anyone to come between us. We used to be able to laugh and talk to each other for hours, without arguing, judging, or hating. Cried on each other's shoulders and could always depend on each other when one of us was in need. Then you married Cedric and things changed. You changed. We felt as if you left us behind because you did. Evelyn got jealous and she did everything in her power to be you and make you pay for what she considers you leaving us. I started to lie about who I was, and my secrets hurt everybody, including my immediate family. I say all of that to say that we've all made some mistakes. Every last one of us, Kayla, so no need to point the finger at one person. I'll let you sit on that for a while. If you choose to come to the hospital, do so. If not, don't. It doesn't matter to me either way, but I also had to make my case for why I believe you should."

Trina gave me a hug then she left. I stood in the kitchen, unsure about what to do. While she made some valid points, still, it was hard for me to go be by Evelyn's side.

For the next couple of hours, I paced the floor and pondered what to do. Things with Cedric, Jacoby, and me were going well, and Jacoby had been spending more time with Cedric. Today they were at a St. Louis University basketball game. I called to see how everything was going.

Jacoby said fine. He hurried to end the call, saying that I was making him miss the game. I was happy about their relationship, but so sad about how my friendship had turned out with Evelyn. Sad enough to change my clothes and head to the hospital.

Before going to Evelyn's room, I stopped by the gift shop to get her a plant and a card. I didn't know why I was so nervous to see her, but I was. I had known her for most of my life, but there I was frightened, as well as hesitant to enter her room. I took a deep breath, before pushing on the door and entering. Instantly, my eyes connected with Evelyn's. She was sitting up in bed with her hair all over her head. Trina sat in a chair next to her with a book in her hand. A wide smile grew on her face, and the smile caused me to display a little grin too.

"Hello," I said, looking from Trina to Evelyn. "I hope I'm not interrupting."

"No, you aren't," Trina said. "I was just reading Evelyn this good book. Girl, it's juicy, drama filled, and hilarious. You may want to come in, sit down, and listen to this."

I walked farther into the room and set the plant in the windowsill.

"Yes, what Trina said is true," Evelyn added. "But good book or not, please stay. It's good to see you."

I cleared mucus from my throat and didn't reply to Evelyn yet. Instead, I walked up to the bed and gave Evelyn the card. She opened it and read my brief message inside that encouraged her to get well soon.

"I'm trying to," she said. "Every day I feel as if I'm getting better. Thanks to Trina for helping me with therapy, and thanks to you, right now, for making me feel as if everything will be okay."

I nodded and took a seat at the end of the bed.

"Can I finish?" Trina said, holding up the book. "At least let me get to the end of this chapter."

"Please do," Evelyn said. "I want to find out what's up."

Trina started to read and we all listened in. We added our opinions about the book, and started conversing with each other more and laughing. That moment took me back to when we were all in the sixth grade. We were laid across the bed in my bedroom, reading books to each other. Had our PJs on and stayed up all night discussing those books, laughing about the characters and wishing that we could be some of them. The books made the characters' lives seem so perfect, especially when our lives were all jacked up. I couldn't help but to feel as if this moment in time was special. Maybe it was the turning point we all needed.

Chapter 20

Evelyn

I had been in the hospital for almost a month. Trina came to see me almost every day, and after that amazing day with my BFF's, Kayla had stopped by several times too. She baked me my favorite: a German chocolate cake with a whole lot of icing. She also helped me with therapy. I was feeling much better and was one day away from going home. While I was definitely looking forward to it, I wasn't looking forward to my uphill court battle with Bryson. From what Trina had said, he was ready to fight me all the way in court. His wealthy parents had hired some of the best lawyers in St. Louis for his defense.

As for me, I couldn't afford an attorney. I had spent a substantial amount of the money Bryson had given me. Somehow, he got a hold of my banking information and withdrew the rest of my money. There was no question that the whole case would be interesting. I had a lot of solid evidence against Bryson that could prove he was guilty. But I was well aware that the attorneys his parents hired would tear my evidence apart and make me look like a thirsty, gold-digging whore. There was a chance I would come out on the losing end.

It was getting late. I sat in bed, finishing the yucky dinner that I hadn't finished earlier. As I ate my peas, I glanced at the numerous cards Kayla and Trina had given me. Kayla's plant had already started to grow, but Trina's balloon had deflated. I smiled while thinking about their kindness. I had to admit that my BFF's had come through for me this time. Never did I think we'd be able to repair all the damage that had been done, but putting everything else aside, it seemed as if we were well on our way to being the good friends we used to be, many years ago.

I finished my dinner and pushed the table away from the bed. Fluffed my pillow and then lay back to get comfortable. I felt myself fading a little, but when the door squeaked open, I widened my eyes to see who it was. From the shadowy figure, I could tell it was a man. My heart started to slam against my chest and beat faster. I thought it was Bryson, coming to finish what he'd started. Instead, it was Cedric. Seeing him put me a little at ease, but after him beating my ass, he was still considered one of my enemies.

He had a card in his hand and a smile was washed across his face. "Hey there, stranger," he said walking farther into the room. "Baby, how are you feeling?"

Baby my ass. Save it, I thought. "Better," was all I said, trying to keep our conversation short.

Cedric laid the card on the table then sat in the chair beside my bed. He crossed his legs and massaged his hands together. "So, when are you getting out of this place?" he asked.

My tone was very nasty. "In a few days. Why?"

"Because I kind of miss my partner in crime. Kind of need you to handle some things for me, and if you do, there will be some great rewards."

I was slumped down in the bed, but sat up to give him my full attention. "What kind of things do you want me to handle? And, I'd like to hear more about those rewards."

Cedric passed me an envelope and asked me to open the letter to read it. It was a letter from Paula Daniels, the woman I thought had attempted to kill him. According to the letter, she wanted to speak to Cedric ASAP about Jacoby's involvement. That was all she said, but she also assured him that everything wasn't what it seemed to be.

I slowly folded the letter and gave it back to Cedric. I wasn't sure what was going on, but I asked Cedric why he couldn't handle this.

"Jacoby is fragile and Kayla is weak. I don't want to hurt anybody's feelings, plus I'm always being lied to. That's why I need you. I need someone like you to check things out for me, and since Kayla is back on your team, maybe you can find out what's really going on for me."

A part of me didn't want to be used by Cedric again, but I still wanted to hear about those rewards. "If I do get involved, what's in this for me?"

"Depends."

"Depends on what?"

"Depends on what you want or what you need. Like a lawyer to help you fight your case, a new house, sex, whatever you want."

"Hmmm, but you haven't said the magic word yet. The one thing that energizes me and turns me into the woman I always wanted to be. A rich woman."

Cedric snapped his finger and smiled. "Oh yeah, that's right. I almost forgot and how could I forget about that. Money, right? However much your heart desires, as long as it's within reason."

I laughed and shot him a slow wink. "It's a good thing that you know me so well, Cedric. But let me think about this. When I get out of here, I'll definitely be in touch."

Cedric stood and straightened his suit jacket. He licked his lips then moved closer to the bed. He leaned in and planted a wet kiss on my cheek. Saying nothing else, he strutted to the door. It slammed behind him.

I, on the other hand, sat with a huge smile on my face, thinking about my best way forward.

BOOK CLUB QUESTIONS

1. Who did you think shot Cedric? Why and were you correct or surprised?
2. To what extent do you think Jacoby is involved in Cedric's attempted murder case?
3. If you were in Kayla's shoes, would you have divorced Cedric? Why or why not?
4. What do you think of Trina and Keith's relationship? Will they survive?
5. What would you do if you were in Kayla's situation? Would you tell Cedric about Jacoby's involvement, considering how Cedric is?
6. If you had a friend like Evelyn, what would you suggest to her?
7. Would you be able to forgive a friend who had sex with your husband and got pregnant by him? If yes, why? If no, why?
8. If you found an open box of condoms in your significant other's possession, know-

ing that you were unaware of them, how would you handle it?

9. What would you do if you discovered your sibling was on the down low?

10. Trina and Kayla struggled with forgiving Evelyn. Would you? Why or why not?

11. How do you feel about women who continue in relationships with men who cheat?

12. Bryson's secret is now out. Who was more wrong for telling his business? Evelyn, Trina, or should Bryson have been honest and told his family and friends?